FATAL CATCH

FATAL CATCH

By

Roxe Anne Peacock

ROXE ANNE PEACOCK
www.roxeannepeacock.com

This book is in *memory* of my wonderful mother Dorothy, brother Maynard and Aunt Viola.
A special thanks to my sisters Kris and Nancy.

Acknowledgments

Endless appreciation goes to my talented, patient co-editors, Heather G. Land and Cecile Kahr.

A special thanks to my wonderful daughter and cover artist, Heather G. Land for the perfect book cover.

And a huge thanks to my friends, Eleonora di Liscia, Susie Curtiss, and Linda Bloom for their support in my writing.

Chapter One

On June 12, 1963 we are sitting in the living room waiting up for Daddy when someone knocks on our door at two in the morning. Mama peers out the door window to see who is at our door at this late hour. Daddy never knocks.

A police car is in our driveway and the Chief of Police, Riley Bennett is standing at our door. Mama opens the door a crack and she tells him she doesn't want to hear anything he has to say; especially about Daddy who hasn't returned home.

Chief Riley tells us kids we best go to our rooms so he can have a word alone with Mama, but we aren't leaving her alone.

The Chief makes Mama sit in a chair and gently reaches for her hand. "Dot," he says. Her real name is Dody Canfield, but everyone around these parts calls her Dot.

"Dot…Daniel's car smashed into a telephone pole by the old swing bridge. He died instantly. There are skid marks, but no one seems to have witnessed the accident. I'm sorry."

Mama stood to walk the Chief to the door. I guess her feet

couldn't hold her up under all the pressure. She just collapses into Chief Riley's arms. It isn't long before the Chief comes around to comfort Mama every day. She says we can just call the Chief, Uncle Riley.

Mama might be petite and only weigh 95 pounds soaking wet, but she can out-fish almost everyone around Grand Detour, Illinois. When Daddy mysteriously died in that car crash leaving her to raise us three kids by herself, fishing becomes a necessity.

Since Daddy's death, my little brother Billie, who just turned nine, always looks sad. He had been Daddy's little man. At first, Mama takes him fishing as much as she can to cheer him up, then she gets too busy with entertaining Uncle Riley.

Billie has short dishwater blond hair with a cowlick in the front. His ears stick out like Dumbo's so Mama tapes them to his head. Billie does a lot of fussing about the tape. He says it pulls his hair. When Mama isn't looking, he takes the tape off right quick. It doesn't seem to help much anyway.

Today is July 10, 1964 and hotter than the blazes. We are too poor to have air conditioning. We only have one squeaky old fan and it is in Mama's bedroom. She says it's hotter in her bedroom than any of the other rooms, so she needs it more. Us kids' bedrooms are upstairs, and it is hotter than the devil up there.

Uncle Riley hasn't been coming around much anymore. Mama told him she needs some time alone with us. She really doesn't spend much time alone; she spends it with another new uncle, Frank Billings. This time our new uncle looks a little older and the top of his head is as shiny as a new bowling ball. It looks like he doesn't get much exercise either since his stomach hangs over his belt. His eyes bug out so much they make him look like a goldfish I once saw in a Dime store. And he has the biggest lips I ever did see. They remind me of the candy wax ones I purchase at Halloween. I don't know what Mama sees in him. I liked Uncle Riley much better even if Mama spent more time with him than us kids.

"Missy, why don't you take Billie to the river and let him fish?" Mama winks at our new uncle just before she gives him a big smooch on his big fat lips. "I won't have time today. Katie can't take him fishing; she has to babysit the neighbor's kids."

If Mama knew the real reason my sister Katie likes babysitting, she would put a stop to it right quick. Ever since Katie turned sixteen, Billie and I are the last people she wants to spend time with. She is too busy kissing her boyfriend, Charlie Goodman.

My name is Missy Canfield and at barely thirteen, I feel more like Billie's Mama than his sister. Mama spends all her time on our new uncle's lap; in Daddy's favorite red velvet chair of all places. She just sits on his lap kissing him until their faces are as chapped as my hands after throwing snowballs in the wintertime.

"Missy, did you hear what I asked you?"

"I heard! You know I don't like taking those fish off the hook by myself."

"Take some pliers with or just cut the line. And, Missy, stay gone until supper."

It seems like it is taking us forever to walk the eight blocks to the river in this heat. With Mama lecturing me, I forgot to pack some Kool-Aid to drink and we don't dare go back home now.

The heat never seems to bother Billie. He just keeps on skipping down the road; picking up a few rocks here and there to throw.

I like to fish, but I hate putting those darn worms on the hook. They smell awful and just keep on wiggling off the hook as fast as I get them on.

Mama got a staph infection once from getting stuck by a catfish fin. She couldn't work for a week. The doctor said, "Dot, if you aren't careful with them fish, the next time you might lose your hand." I've been afraid of getting horned by those fish ever since.

The Rock River looks like an oil painting today. It gives me such a peaceful feeling hearing the river current rushing against the dock, frogs croaking, and meadow larks warbling in the distance. I'm glad this is one of Billie's favorite places to fish, if I have to take him fishing.

"Missy, can we fish by the boats tied to the dock?" he asks, pointing down the hill.

"I suppose," I reply.

"Oh boy...thanks!"

"Promise me you won't fall in, Mama will kill us if we come home all muddy and wet." Mumbling, I continue. "She should be taking you fishing instead of sitting in Daddy's chair kissing Uncle Frank."

"Did you say something, Missy?"

"Forget it. It wasn't important."

The water looks inviting. Sweat is dripping off my blonde hair forming ringlets and seeping under my blue, pointy rimmed frames causing my eyes to sting. Mama says my eyes are the color of Daddy's. I'm happy about my eyes, but I sure wish I hadn't inherited Daddy's pale skin. The rest of my family is sure lucky. They are as tan as the new rawhide purse Uncle Frank purchased for Mama.

I set Billie's pole and tackle box down on the steaming hot dock. I can't get my shoes off fast enough. The gentle waves smacking my feet in the cool, murky river water is sure going to feel good. I just hope nothing nibbles on my toes thinking they are bait. Crabs, minnows, and bluegill hang out around the dock and boats. And since someone left their boat tied to this dock, there might be more than usual.

It's fun sitting on the dock, but I'd rather be sitting in the shade under a weeping willow tree reading a good book instead of baiting Billie's hook every five minutes. He can't seem to keep his pole in the water long enough to catch a nibble.

I bait Billie's hook with a big, fat, slimy night crawler. It sure wiggles as I push it further on the hook. Something smells real bad, too. It smells like someone left a bunch of dead fish on the river bank to smolder in the hot sun for days. The flies seem to be biting worse than normal, and there seems to be twice as many.

"Missy, how come I haven't had any nibbles? We've been here a real long time. Do you have any vanilla to put on my worm? Mama says vanilla is her secret for catching a lot of fish. She says fish can smell the vanilla a mile away."

"No, Billie, I think the only person in the world who carries vanilla while fishing is Mama. For goodness sake, don't keep reeling your pole in and throwing it back out. You're never going to catch a fish! Be patient for once and stop rocking this dock, you're making me dizzy. The fish can hear everything going on and you are going to scare their tails right off of them. The fish are probably half baked by now. I know I am."

Not a sound can be heard except for Billie's complaining. Our town doesn't have much traffic, and there isn't anyone else around except for the occasional boat passing by. I begin fanning myself with my hands in hopes of catching some of the breeze which occasionally blows our way. It is too hot today for a fire-breathing dragon.

Billie reels his pole in just as a pontoon boat passes by on the opposite side of the river bank.

"Missy, Missy, I've got a fish. It's a big one. It must be a whale! Please help me reel it in. I don't think I can get it in by myself. It's too big. It doesn't seem to be moving at all. I don't want to lose my fish. It is the biggest fish anyone's probably caught in their whole life!" Billie shouts with excitement. "It's Old Moe, the granddaddy of all fish! Won't Mama be surprised if I catch her Old Moe?"

Old Moe is a legend around these parts of the country. Everyone has seen Old Moe at one time or another. The person who catches Old Moe is going to be the luckiest person in the world. Old Moe is actually a twenty or twenty-five pound carp that almost everyone in our county has provided a snack to. He just takes a small bite off your bait, and then jumps out of the water to see who is teasing him. Some of the old-time fishermen are going to be really disappointed if Billie does have him on his hook and lands him. Mama, of course, will be real proud of her little man. Daddy would be proud if he were alive, too. Mama will be able to go to the bars and brag about Billie outdoing fishermen around these parts for miles. She might even give them her special grin and wink like she always does. I've seen her give it to our new uncles enough.

"Billie, hand me your pole fast, and keep reeling in as you do! We don't want to lose this fish now, do we?" *I am secretly hoping to land Old Moe myself.*

Billie hands me his pole just as I instructed. I can tell he has something really big on the end of his line. If it isn't Old Moe, it might just be an old log under the mud. I can feel whatever it is move once in a while, but I can't see it. I've been trying to land Billie's fish for at least twenty minutes. Bubbles are beginning to come up from the bottom of the river. Sweat is dripping down my face once again causing my eyes to sting. The heat must be causing me to hallucinate. *I have to be brave for my little brother's sake.* My legs buckle. From the look on Billie's face; he must see what is in the water, too.

Billie points to the end of his line and screams. "Missy, that's no fish. It looks like a...a...don't reel it in. I want to go home! Let's run, Missy. Please?"

"No, Billie, we have to see what is at the other end of this hook."

The bubbles steadily are getting larger. The more I reel in, I can see something coming to the surface of the murky water. "Maybe it's our reflection," I tell Billie.

"Uh, I don't think it looks like me."

The closer the object comes to the surface, I see what resembles a man's face; his eyes wide open and staring at us. It looks like a night crawler someone left on their hook for days and kept in the water for just as long; all swollen, no color, and pure white. My stomach is churning, and my mouth is producing way too much saliva. I hope I don't throw up all over this dock and in the water with the corpse.

"Missy, what are we going to do? We're going to go to jail. We killed him! We killed him right here at this very dock. Just like the bird you killed last year fishing!" Billie says matter of fact.

"Billie, calm down. We didn't kill anyone! Let me think for a minute." I sit on the dock holding Billie's fishing line tight. "Maybe he isn't dead. Maybe he's just hurt. And if we get help real fast, he'll be okay. We have to tell someone. We aren't going to jail. I promise!

"I'm not sure who we are going to tell." *I suspect Mama wants more alone time with Uncle Frank. Katie is babysitting. It wouldn't be good for little kids to see the gruesome face in the river. Everyone we know with a telephone lives too far. I don't know who I'm afraid of more, the lifeless body in the water or Mama.*

"I'm scared!"

"I know…I know!"

Our small town doesn't have a real fire station. The nearest police station is over in Dixon. The little grocery store, Candy's General Store, is about a mile away from where we are fishing. It has the only pay phone in town except for the bars, and we aren't allowed in them anyway except with Mama. And we don't have any money with us.

"Billie, run to the fire station and tell the firemen to come to the dock down the hill by the willow tree. And, Billie, tell them a man is drowning in the river!"

"What if they don't believe me? I'm just a little kid," he cries.

"Just tell them I'm at the dock waiting."

I watch him run as fast as his little feet can take him. I sure hope he watches for cars if any come down the road. I am supposed to be babysitting him and not let him out of my sight. I hope Mama understands.

My arms are getting tired from holding on to Billie's fishing pole so tightly in fear of losing the man forever. It seems like a lifetime since Billie went for help. Finally, I can hear sirens coming from all directions. I have never heard a better sound.

A fireman runs down the hill to the dock toward me. He quickly looks the situation over. "Young lady, show me what you and your brother have found."

"I'm Missy, sir, and Billie and I were just fishing on the dock when he thought he had the biggest fish ever on his line. I tried helping him reel his fish in. The more I reeled and tugged on the line, the more we could tell we didn't have a fish. We saw an outline of what seems to be a man's face. He is out there at the end of this fishing line, sir!" I proceed to pull the fishing line even tighter so the fireman can see exactly what is under the water.

Billie begins crying hysterically. "We didn't do anything, sir. Please don't arrest us. We didn't kill anyone. Honest!"

In our town, if sirens are heard, everyone tries to figure out where it is going to see who might be injured or deceased. Everyone except Mama, she is usually too busy entertaining our new uncle.

The fireman wades in the water looking the situation over. I think he is trying to see if the man might still be alive. Police and firemen keep running down the hill to the river with a stretcher and other medical equipment. I don't think it's going to help the man.

A fireman came and told us to go up the hill and wait until someone questions us. We did as we were told. We didn't want to see the man's ghastly face ever again. I know I am going to have nightmares. There won't be enough covers to hide my head under.

Billie and I wait for what seems like hours before they bring the body up from the river. One of the man's hands looks all swollen and white. He has a ring on his left hand. The ring looks so tight it looks like it might cut the dead man's finger right off. The coroner, Ned Baily, covers the body with a white sheet. *Thank goodness!*

The police tell everyone to stay back. They are treating the area as a crime scene until an autopsy can be performed.

Billie and I inch closer to hear what the coroner whispers to Uncle Riley. He doesn't do a very good job. He sounds like Billie when he tells secrets.

"Riley, it looks like someone struck the corpse with something hard on his right temple as he was preparing his boat for fishing. This oar has blood on it, and the dead man's boat has dried up bait lying on the bottom by his fishing poles. Nothing seems to be missing. We can rule out robbery."

"Ned, a woman reported her fiancé missing three days ago. The corpse fits the woman's description. If this is the same person, his name is Henry McDougall, a forty-two year-old who owns a hardware store in Dixon. Mr. McDougall looks to be the approximate age and had been wearing the exact gold Celtic ring as the deceased has on."

Uncle Riley walks up to Billie and me. "You don't have to worry. You kids aren't in trouble. No one is going to arrest you. You did the right thing by going for help. This man has been in the water for days and there was nothing you could have done to save him. I'll stop by and talk to your Mama about the incident when I return your fishing pole."

Billie and I slowly walk home. "Missy, do you think the man died instantly like Daddy?"

"I don't know. We did the best we could. You heard Uncle Riley!"

"Yeah, but it doesn't make me feel any better. Do you think the person who killed Henry McDougall will kill us, too?"

I don't want to cause Billie to worry, but I am wondering the same thing myself. "No, the only person I'm worried about at the moment is Mama. We're late for supper."

Billie flexes his arm. "If a killer comes after me, I'm going to show him my muscles!"

I start laughing. "Your muscles are pretty big, but I don't think they'd stop a killer."

I know one thing for sure; we aren't going to fish on that dock again. In fact, we aren't going to step on the dock for any reason.

Billie runs into the house before I can stop him.

"Mama, I caught a man on my hook. Don't be mad at us. We didn't kill him. He was already dead!"

"Missy, what is your brother talking about? You kids making up stories again?"

"No, Mama. Billie really did catch a dead man. A lot of police and firemen helped us get him out of the river. I'm sorry we're late for dinner."

"That must have been what all the sirens were for. We kind of wondered about all the ruckus. Did you see Uncle Riley?"

"Yes, he said he'd bring our fishing pole back and have a talk with you when things get settled."

Uncle Frank starts acting strange. He just keeps grinning at Mama's questioning. I have had enough questions for one day. *I sure wish Mama would drop the subject.*

"Was the coroner there?" Uncle Frank asks.

"Yep, someone named Ned showed up. He talked to Uncle Riley for a long time. He told Uncle Riley he was going to rule the dead man's death—what did he call it, Missy?"

"Suspicious."

"Missy, did anyone mention how he died, or where he came from, or maybe his name?"

"Umm—I think the man might have been hit on the head with his boat's oar. And if it had been a robbery, the robber would have taken his fishing tackle and pole," I answer puzzled by his questioning.

Uncle Frank drops into his chair. He doesn't have a grin on his face any longer.

The nightmares come about every other night. I sleep with

the lights on and the covers over my head. I can't get Mr. McDougall's ghastly face out of my mind, and the thought of him possibly being murdered still frightens me. I will have to make sure I keep a close eye on Billie. We might be the killer's next victims if he finds out we found Mr. McDougall's body. *I sure hope he wasn't watching us at the river!*

Chapter Two

Mama calls us to the living room.

"Kids, this is Sammy DelRosa, Uncle Frank's best friend. You can just call him Uncle Sammy. They're both going to live with us from now on!" Mama says in her glory. She will have two men doting on her every word instead of one.

Uncle Sammy has dark-brown, curly hair which matches his brown eyes. He is much better looking than Uncle Frank, but there is something sinister looking about him that makes me shiver. He has a short-sleeved shirt showing off his big tattoo of a skull and crossbones. In the movies, men who wear tattoos are the bad guys.

Uncle Sammy walks over to Katie and begins stroking her long, silky brown hair. "It's a pleasure to meet you Miss Katharine Canfield!"

Katie gingerly inches back away from Uncle Sammy.

Billie and I stay far away from his reach. We don't want him touching us. But we tell him we are glad to meet him so Mama won't get mad.

"Kids, your Uncle Sammy's going to sleep in the guest room. His rent will help pay the grocery bill."

Katie and I look across the room at each other. We will have more house work, and Mama will be kissing our new uncle, Frank, in Daddy's overstuffed chair every night just like she did for a while with Uncle Riley. She'd just sit on his lap kissing and giggling all night long. *I guess Mama likes having an audience.*

Renting to Uncle Sammy is going to cost Mama more in groceries than he pays rent. He looks like he can eat enough for three people and will probably dirty just as many dishes. He must have read our minds. He just keeps winking at Katie and me.

When Mama isn't working at one of her two jobs, she sits around and paints her fingernails. She usually paints them a crimson red.

She wears bright red lipstick to match her fingernails. I think she tries her best to look like Marilyn Monroe. I can't imagine her not having her hair done or her makeup just right. When she smiles, you can see her perfectly straight pearly white teeth. No matter what Mama eats or does, she always looks like a model. *Some people are just born lucky.*

We have an old wringer washer which takes forever to wash our clothes, but at least it works. We can't afford a dryer, so

Mama was thrilled when Daddy put up a clothes line to hang our laundry on. I don't much care for hanging out laundry. It means a lot more work. After we bring in the laundry, we have to iron everything including our new uncles' boxer shorts. I hate men's shorts of any kind. What are the neighbors going to say with us hanging out men's underwear to dry? Mama isn't even married, and there are two men living in our house!

Katie doesn't like Uncle Sammy, and she especially doesn't like ironing his boxers. She says, "Uncle Sammy is always bumping my breasts and teasing me about wanting to get inside his shorts when Mama isn't around. I can't wait for him to find another place to live so he'll leave me alone!"

I might be thirteen but my chest still looks more like the eggs over-easy Mama cooks than breasts. Mama says I'm just a late bloomer and not to get worried. I guess I should be grateful I'm built more like a boy with Uncle Sammy living here. It doesn't stop him from winking at me. I hate him coming too close; he wears too much cologne. Katie says it is what all older men wear; Old Spice.

I wish we had a television set. At night we sit around the living room and do puzzles, play slap jack, rummy or Monopoly. I hate Monopoly! It takes too long to finish a game, and I always lose. I'm real good at rummy.

The living room has the most beautiful field-stone fireplace and mantle. When Daddy was alive, we made popcorn in our fireplace. At Christmas, he put cinnamon sticks and pine cones in the fireplace to make our house smell festive.

When it isn't in use, Mama puts a bronze fireplace screen in front of the opening. She bought it cheap at a garage sale.

Mama sits and sings country western songs in the living room to Uncle Frank. She loves to sing songs by Hank Locklin and Kitty Wells. When she finishes with one song about falling in love, she just starts singing another. Mama sings all her favorite songs to all our new uncles.

Her favorite actor and singer is Elvis Presley. She acts like a teenager when she hears him sing. Once, when Mama went to see one of his new movies at the theater, I thought for sure she was going to faint right there in front of everyone.

Uncle Frank likes Mama's singing. He just grabs her up and swings her around giving her a great big smooch. Our dog, Sandy, always snarls at him. She thinks he is hurting her. And maybe Sandy is a bit jealous. She used to sleep with Mama after Daddy died.

The light is shining bright through the lace curtains in my bedroom window. The sun is reflecting off a prism I have hanging in front of it. Colors of yellow, blue, and red are dancing across my bedroom walls. The brightest red male cardinal is perched on a branch on the tree outside the window. He almost resembles the color of Mama's lipstick.

I decide to go downstairs and make me some cereal to eat out on our porch so I can hear the birds sing. I might even give Sandy some of my milk.

Our house has a faded white picket fence around three

sides. Our back porch is enclosed with large windows and lace curtains at the top. Mama lovingly furnished the porch with white wicker furniture and an old braided rug made by her grandma. She placed a crazy quilt her grandma made out of all her old clothes over a white wicker rocker.

Sometimes Mama just goes out and sits in the rocker doing nothing but smiling. She says the porch reminds her of her grandma. We can enter the porch from our living room. It is one of Sandy's favorite places to lay.

"After breakfast, girl, you want to go see Calico?"

Sandy wags her tail happy to know she gets to see her best friend.

Sandy and I can't wait to go out to our barn and see Calico's kittens. Last year, Sandy brought home a litter of kittens. We don't know where she found them, but she sure thought they were her babies. She even tried nursing them, not that she had any milk.

We kept one of the kittens, a white female with bright orange and black spots. We named her Calico. Sandy and Calico used to do everything together; that is until the neighbor's cat started to come over and sing to Calico all night long. Now Calico has kittens out in our barn. They are the cutest little things I've ever seen. The kittens don't have their eyes open yet, but when they do, you can bet Sandy and I will play with them.

Sandy begins pacing and barking at the door. I look out the window and see Calico eating something. *Good for you, Calico!*

At least you're getting enough food to feed your babies.

"Sandy, it's just Calico. Calm down and drink your milk before Mama sees you."

Sandy continues barking and jumping on the porch door to go out. "Calm down, girl. I'll open the door for you, but leave Calico alone!"

As I open the door, Sandy flies past me. "Sandy, I told you to—What in the world do you have, Calico?"

I run after Sandy trying to keep her from stealing Calico's catch. "Oh, Calico, what do you have in your mouth? Oh, no. I'm sorry! What happened to your baby?"

"Mama, come quick! Calico has something in her mouth."

Mama walks out on the porch wiping her hands on her apron. "She's probably moving her kittens because you two won't leave her alone. I told you not to bother her!"

"No, Mama, it's just a head—no body!" I point at Calico's mouth. "Look, she has a kitten's head in her mouth!" I cry.

We walk over to Calico to see what she really has. I sure hope it isn't one of her babies. That is exactly what it is! Mama and I run to the barn.

"Maybe you had better stay back, Missy. In case something is wrong."

Mama puts her arm around me. "Missy, all of Calico's kittens are dead! Sometimes animals dispose of their young when something is wrong with them."

I jerk away from Mama's reach. "I don't care. How can any living thing do something so awful to their babies? I hate

Calico!"

I run to the house crying. I can barely see the porch. I begin puking my guts out. I can't get the horrible image of Calico holding one of her kitten's heads in her mouth out of my head.

Mama brings me a cool wash cloth and places it on my forehead. "Missy, are you going to be okay?"

"I think I'll have to sleep with the lights on for a while. And I never want to see Calico again!"

Mama takes Calico for a long ride. She never wants to see her again either. Uncle Frank is glad all of the cats are gone. He just leans against the front door smiling at Mama and Calico as they leave our driveway.

For a time, Sandy lays by our barn waiting for her cat to return home. She won't eat a thing. After a few days of starving, she comes to her senses. She eats everything in sight and doesn't leave Mama's side; which doesn't make Uncle Frank happy.

Chapter Three

"Missy, would you like to go to the park with me and my friends," Katie asks.

Katie takes me by surprise. She never asks me to go with her and her friends. Once her interests turned to boys, she spends her spare time painting her nails and rolling her hair in huge rollers. She looks like someone from outer space!

Katie and her boyfriend, Charlie Goodman, came up with a plan for when she babysits. She dials his number and lets it ring three times. This means she has put the kids to bed so he can come over. I suspect they spend their time alone on the couch kissing like Mama and Uncle Frank. She doesn't need any practice in this area; she has peeked enough at Mama and Uncle Frank to get the idea.

"Are we going to have a picnic?" I ask curious.

"No, we're just going out for a ride and we might play a little baseball," Katie snickers.

I put my hair up in a ponytail with a baby blue ribbon tied

to it. I choose my best pair of shorts; blue checked and to my knees. It should go nicely with my favorite white cotton shirt with an embroidered butterfly in the middle. Most of our clothes come from garage sales or our cousins. The only time we get something new might be for our birthdays or Christmas. The clothes we wear are usually a couple of sizes too big or too short. Some even have holes in them before we get to wear them. The worst is when I have to wear boy's clothes. But at least they are always clean.

The only shoes I have are made of white canvas, which now look gray and have a hole at the right big toe. We wear bobby socks most of the time. Actually, I prefer to go barefoot. Mama can't afford to buy us kids' new shoes very often. She says, "If your feet grow any more, I'll have to buy you skis; they'll last longer. When I went to school I had to walk five miles even if my shoes were too tight or had holes in them. Sometimes I even had to go barefoot. You kids should be glad you even have shoes as poor as we are!"

Charlie picks us up in his 1957 red and white Chevy. He must have been shining his car all morning. We stop and pick up a couple more of their friends on our way to the park. The car sure is crowded.

We play baseball for what seems like an eternity. I'm not good at playing any type of ball. I got hit in the face with a hard ball once, and my face swelled all up.

"Missy, I'm not bringing you anymore. You embarrass me.

Either catch the ball or go sit down, you big coward. If you catch it, it won't hit you in the face!"

"Katie, I'm too hot. I don't want to play anymore. No one has thrown the ball my direction for a long time. I'm just standing around most of the time."

"If you didn't duck, someone might throw the ball to you. Just go and be a baby, and sit down somewhere. I should have brought Billie!"

"You should have brought Billie. I'm sick of waiting for you to be done!" I yell, stomping to a nearby tree. I sure wish I'd brought my new Bobbsey Twins book to read. I have been sitting under this oak tree for so long the sun is starting to go down and it's beginning to cool off. *I wish we had packed us a picnic. I'm pretty hungry, and it is way past supper by now. My stomach is growling.*

"Katie, when are we going home? Mama will be mad we missed supper. It's starting to get dark. You can't even see the ball when it comes your way!" I complain.

"Stop being a baby. The game's almost finished!" She yells.

If I had known we were going to be gone this long, I would have brought along a sweater to keep myself warm. Bringing my knees to my chest and putting my arms inside my shirt makes me feel a bit warmer. One thing about the weather in the Midwest, the days can be hotter than blazes, but at dusk it might just cool down quick.

Katie and her friends begin laughing and carrying on. *I wish I knew what was so funny.* They must be up to something to be whispering and carrying on like gossiping girls. Maybe they are all making fun of me for ducking. *I guess I'll find out what the joke is soon enough.*

"We have to go home. Mama will be worried sick, and she has to leave for work soon. She'll ground us for sure, and it won't even be my fault!"

Katie gives me an evil look like I am going to get it when she gets me alone. I've seen that look many times before.

Everyone begins piling into the crowded Chevy. All of us are crammed into the car like jelly in a doughnut. The boys smell worse than catfish guts on a river bank. I try holding my breath for as long as I can. All of Katie's friends are roaring with laughter and staring at me. *I wish I could be at any other place but in the back seat of Charlie's Chevy.*

"Missy, we are going to stop somewhere before we go home. We want to show you something!" Katie begins laughing.

"But we have to go home!" I protest.

"I'll just tell Mama we stopped to pick up my babysitting money. You know Mama never gets mad when it comes to making money!"

We start driving up the hill toward the town's small cemetery, Grand Oak. I have heard stories from my friends at school about the cemetery being haunted. You never want to go there after dark. There is a rumor about a young girl from our town visiting her grandmother's grave and never being seen again. I never want any part of any cemetery day or night. There aren't even any stars out yet, and I can't see much of the moon either.

The sky has a dark eerie look to it. The wind is blowing ever so lightly; making it sound like someone whispering. *I wish I was home in my own bed with the covers over my head.*

We stop at the middle of the cemetery. My heart feels like it is going to beat right out of my chest.

"Why are we here? I want to go home! I want to go right now, please?"

Katie points to an object towering above all the other dimly lit tombstones. "Missy, we're just going to walk a little ways over to that tombstone. I have a surprise for you. I will give it to you when we get there; if you're not a coward. Missy, you'll love it. Trust me. It will be fun!"

"Nothing about this cemetery looks fun to me, Katie Canfield!"

The boys begin laughing. Terrified, I will my feet to move toward the huge structure. My body is chilled to the bone just thinking about what might be lurking behind it.

"Close your eyes, Missy. When you open them, you'll see your surprise!" Katie instructs.

I close my eyes anticipating the worst. My heart is clean up in my throat. I'm trying to take deep, slow breaths, but it isn't helping. After what seems like a lifetime, I slowly open first one eye and then the next. There isn't a soul to be seen. Darkness is suffocating me. The only sound I hear is the whispering of the wind coming from all directions. I can't stop shaking, and I am so hungry I could eat catfish bait!

I collapse beside the tall tombstone; placing my hands inside my shirt to keep warm. And then I begin crying until there are no tears left to fall onto my damp shirt.

When my senses return and I get up the courage, I begin searching for Katie and her mean friends. Their playing pranks on me has gone too far this time. Maybe they are watching me squirm from behind another tombstone; snickering and carrying on. *I'll show them. I'm not going to cry like a baby again so they can make fun of me for the rest of my life!*

Katie has played her last prank on me. I'll show her I'm not going to be such an easy target from now on; if my lily white skin isn't glowing in the dark for Dracula to find!

Sometimes Katie convinces Billie to help her hold me down. They tickle me until it hurts. And when she babysits, she turns the light to the upstairs off as I'm climbing the stairs. I swear she loves hearing me scream.

But this is the last straw! The next time old Uncle Sammy tries bumping into her, I'm going to make myself invisible. She'll have to find someone else to come to her rescue.

"Katie…Charlie, are you guys out there? This is not funny. Please! I will do anything you want. I will do the dishes for two weeks and make your bed. Come on. I'm cold and hungry!"

No one answers. Katie and her friends left me out here to die. I can't see my hand in front of my face. *Which way did we come in? I'll never find my way out!* I lie down by the nearest tombstone, curl up into a fetal position and put my arms inside my shirt. If I go to sleep and make it through the night alive, I will get even with her tomorrow!

When I wake up, the sun is shining bright through my lace curtains. The male cardinal is sitting on a branch outside my window again. If I had the window open, I could almost touch him. The heat from the sun feels wonderful beating on my face. Today is going to be a glorious day. I am going to get even with Katharine Canfield if it is the last thing I do!

When I arrive in the kitchen for breakfast, Mama is there waiting for me. I'm sure she's going to want all the details of last evening. And I want to know how I got home. Mama looks tired which means someone is in big trouble. She didn't even curl her hair with bobby pins as usual. And she looks madder than a raccoon with rabies!

"Missy, how did you end up at the cemetery last night? Why weren't you home before dark? You know I'm too tired after working all night to be playing these games with you kids. What in the blazes got into you? You better have some answers young lady, and I want them now!" Mama begins crying.

Mama always cries when she is angry. Someone is about to get it and get it good. From the look on her face, I best begin talking and fast. Believe me; I'm not going to forget any details!

I begin with the baseball game and keep on talking until I

got to the part about Katie kissing Charlie. I especially don't want to leave the kissing out. Katie is going to be in horse manure right up to her elbows for kissing him!

Uncle Frank leans in closer to me when I begin talking about Katie kissing. *He sure is a pervert. He's almost as bad as Uncle Sammy. Maybe this is the reason they are best friends.*

After I finish telling Mama about Charlie, I kind of figured he wouldn't be coming around the house for a while to help Katie pull pranks on me. And poor Katie, she'll have to walk to babysitting from now on. She won't be sitting in Charlie's shiny 1957 Chevy for quite a while. She will be putty in my hands!

Mama glares at Katie. "You know Missy is afraid of the dark! How could you do this to your sister, Katharine Canfield?"

"Charlie and the rest of the kids thought it would be funny to watch Missy try to find her way out of the cemetery. We all know she's a baby about everything. And, Mama, Missy needs to get over her fear of the dark!"

"You're grounded for two weeks. You aren't to leave the yard, and absolutely no one is to come over to visit you. Don't you even think of using the phone! Do you understand me?"

"Yes, Mama, I understand."

"Oh, and Katie, you can do Missy's share of the chores!"

"But, Mama…."

"Katie, I don't ever want to hear about you kissing Charlie while babysitting again. That isn't in the job description, and it isn't what you are getting paid for!"

I wish I could have handed out the punishment for Katie instead of Mama. I would have added cleaning the bathrooms, scrubbing windows, and ironing all of Uncle Frank's and Uncle Sammy's boxers.

Uncle Frank begins looking at Katie strangely after the cemetery prank. Mama keeps telling him he ought not to be looking at Katie that way. This has caused quite a few arguments between them lately.

Since Mama grounded Katie, she had to miss out on Charlie's 17th birthday party. She heard all the details from one of her friends who stopped by the house when Mama wasn't home. Charlie took a freshman to his party as a date. The girl has real long, curly auburn hair and a figure like an hour glass. Her family is one of the richest families in Grand Detour. Katie went to her bedroom and cried all night. She didn't even come down for supper. Of course, Mama kept her word and made Katie come down to do the dishes. Immediately after, Katie went back to our bedroom. I almost feel sorry for her.

Uncle Sammy is trying more than ever to brush up against Katie's chest area. He must have heard from Uncle Frank about her kissing Charlie. I pretend to look the other way when he is around. *Maybe Katie will think twice about needling me again!*

Just as I anticipate, I begin having nightmares about being

back at the cemetery. There are no stars shining or a bright moon to light up the sky. The air is brisk and damp. A man with no teeth just grins at me from behind a tombstone. The man's bald head glows in the dark. An empty grave has a tombstone engraved with my name on it. Someone keeps calling my name. "Missy...Missy it's too bad your Mama didn't arrive in time to save you. It didn't take long for my hands to squeeze the life out of you. Now you can join your dead daddy. Come with me!"

Just as the man reaches out to pull me towards him, I wake from my dream. The nightmares continue a couple times a week. Every time the toothless man reaches for me, I wake up. It takes hours for me to close my eyes in fear of resuming the dream.

Katie told me that once, when Mama sent Uncle Frank to pick her up from babysitting, she saw him peeping through the living room window at her and Charlie. She said he grinned so much he looked like a pumpkin at Halloween. Old Uncle Frank never said a word to her all the way home. He just drove in silence with an evil look on his face. *One day Uncle Frank will slip up and Mama will see just how evil he is!*

Several weeks later I had the same dream. Mama tells me in the morning I went into her and Uncle Frank's bedroom and began hitting him as hard as I could. She said Uncle Frank wanted to pop me right there on the spot. Lucky for me, Mama convinced him I was sleepwalking. She had Uncle

Frank carry me upstairs to bed without waking me. She told him it wasn't good to wake someone when they are sleepwalking.

Billie and Katie got a tickle out of me smacking Uncle Frank. I thought they would never stop laughing. Uncle Frank turns toward me and gives me an evil look.

"I should have just left you out in the dark cemetery for someone to bury you, Missy Canfield!"

Funny thing is I never had the dream again after I hit old Uncle Frank.

Chapter Four

Mama and Uncle Frank go out to the local bars quite often. At first, they are happy; even seem like teenagers; kissing and holding hands. Mama always gets dressed up in the clothes Uncle Frank buys her. He brings her presents of jewelry, shoes, new clothes, and skimpy, silky nighties. Uncle Frank always tells Mama he wants his girl to be the prettiest girl in town.

Mama says Uncle Frank's pampering makes her feel like a princess. I'm sure he has the money to purchase extravagant presents; he isn't paying any rent or buying groceries.

I overheard Uncle Frank tell Mama once that he wants her to look like the nude portrait of the beautiful woman he purchased hanging in their bedroom. He even bought her a fancy chenille bedspread to match the color of the background of the picture. Just the thought of old Uncle Frank saying this to Mama makes me want to puke.

After a few months of bliss, Mama and Uncle Frank leave

the house to go out for dinner and drinks. By the time they return home, they are completely drunk. They can barely walk. The minute they get out of the car they begin screaming and cursing at each other so loud, people in the next town can probably hear them. They are calling each other horrible names; some I haven't ever heard before. At least I never heard Mama call my Daddy those names!

"Frank, you dirty bastard; I hate you! You make me sick. Don't ever embarrass me again in front of my friends. Roger always puts his arm around all the girls when he has been drinking. He doesn't mean anything by it. He is one of my best customers at the restaurant. Leave him alone. You didn't have to push him into the pool table!"

"He was kissing your cheek and hanging all over you. You are supposed to be my girl, not some slut! If I ever see Roger touching you again, he will lose that arm he puts around your neck. And if I see him kissing you, he might turn up dead!"

"I don't belong to you or any man! Do you understand me? I can take care of myself. I have been taking care of the kids and myself since Dan died."

"I'm sorry, Dot. I love you. Please forgive me?"

"I'll forgive you this time, but don't you ever touch Roger again."

They leave for bed laughing and carrying on as if nothing happened. I sat at the upstairs register staring down into the now dark kitchen; wondering if Uncle Frank really would kill Roger.

Katie, Billie, and I hate the mornings after Mama and Uncle Frank go out. They sleep until noon and we aren't to disturb them. In fact, Mama told us to stay in bed until they get up. We learn to read a lot on those mornings. I sure can't wait until school starts!

A couple of days later, Uncle Frank brings Mama a fuzzy, brown stuffed teddy bear with bendable arms and legs. It has a beautiful big crimson red bow tied around its neck.

"Dot, this bear is to remind you of how much I love you when I'm not here!"

Uncle Frank makes Mama melt like an ice cream cone in the desert. She plants the biggest smooch on him I ever did see.

"Oh, Frank, I told you I forgave you. You sure are a big teddy bear yourself. I love you, Frank Billings!"

Yuck, I don't know what Mama sees in a man who calls her names and doesn't pay rent. If she wants a teddy bear so badly, maybe us kids can buy her one.

Every few weeks when Mama has a weekend off from bartending and cooking at Dixon Inn and Victory Bar & Gill, we get to go camping at Castle Rock. It is only a few miles away. Castle Rock is a huge rock that overlooks the Rock River. Some say Black Hawk used to sit on top of the big rock to watch for settlers. There are even caves at the top. I have never seen anything so beautiful in my life.

Trailers sit at the bottom of Castle Rock which people rent

for the summer. In front of the trailers is the most fantastic view of the Rock River. Sometimes you can even see deer drinking in the river. Camping there brings back wonderful memories of when Daddy was still alive.

On the other side of the hill at the bottom of Castle Rock, there is Castle Rock Restaurant and Bar. It has the best fried catfish for miles, except Mama's. On the weekends they have live entertainment; mostly country western bands. Mama and Uncle Frank are frequent visitors of the bar just like Daddy was before he died. The bar is where Daddy introduced Mama to Uncle Frank and Uncle Sammy. *I sure wish he hadn't done that.*

My Aunt May, Uncle Jimmy, and twin cousins Rita and Bobby who are both twelve, all camp at Castle Rock on and off during the summer months. Their trailer is only three doors down from ours.

As soon as we arrive at our campground, we set up the volleyball net. Unfortunately for us kids the adults have to have a few beers first. They stumble all over each other trying to hit the ball. When the women fall, they sit on the ground giggling like a bunch of teenagers.

The next morning, they all complain they hurt. They barely move. I think part of their problem is they have hangovers. We kids could have told them they were too old to be acting like children.

Before breakfast, Mama and Uncle Frank set cane poles out all up and down the river bank. They hold up their poles with branches that resemble forks. Every few hours Mama and Uncle Frank check to see if their poles still have bait on them or if they have a fish on the end of their line. This is the lazy way to fish if you ask me. Once in a great while they pull in a catfish or bullhead. If Uncle Jimmy is lucky, he might even have a turtle at the end of his line. Turtle is his favorite food to eat and our favorite entertainment if he lets us play with it first.

My cousins, Rita and Bobby, brought along huge flat pieces of cardboard for all of us so we could go sledding on a steep grassy hill. Billie, Rita, Bobby, and I climb to the top of the steep hill and use our cardboard pieces as sleds. The higher the grass, the faster we fly down the hill. Once we wear the grass down to the dirt, we move to a new location. The grassy areas are great for the first couple days, then it becomes way too short and the cardboard doesn't slide. We just go down the hill like an inchworm.

"Hey, I'm tired of sledding. You want to climb to the top of Castle Rock and carve our initials with today's date?" Billie asks.

We all go in our trailers and put tennis shoes on to climb the steep rocks. Once we reach the top, I sure take my shoes off right quick. I want to feel the warm sand between my toes.

"Hey, anyone want to play cowboys and Indians?" Billie asks.

I am usually the Indian. They get the caves for their hide-outs.

We all pretend it is in the early 1800's. The Indian scouts sit on the highest part of the rock scouting for covered wagons and riders on horseback. Sometimes we pretend the boats on the river are canoes.

We can see for miles up and down the Rock River and through the woods on the steep cliffs. Billie always wants to be a cowboy. All of us kids begin running and jumping from one steep rock to another not worrying about how many hundreds of feet it is to the bottom of Castle Rock.

Katie calls us all over to a smooth rock. "Hey, you guys want to hear the story of Chief Black Hawk first?"

Billie is the first to arrive. He sits down next to her quickly before anyone else can. "I want to hear about Black Hawk!"

Katie has seen a lot of westerns at the movies and knows a little bit of the local history about Black Hawk from her teacher at school. She begins telling us about the great chief.

"Chief Black Hawk was born right here in Illinois; in an Indian village near the mouth of the Rock River. He was born a Pottawattamie, but later became a chief of the Sacs and Foxes. Some say he was born a chief. He only had one wife whom he loved and cherished. He told everyone she was a good wife. Most Indians never talked about their women."

"Katie, I don't want to hear the mushy stuff. I get enough of it from Mama and Uncle Frank. Just tell us about the fighting!" Billie says, wrinkling up his face.

"Okay, but I kind of like the idea Black Hawk only loved one woman. It is romantic!"

Leave it up to Katie to think of romance. Her favorite

movie is Beauty and the Beast. Uncle Frank and Mama ruined romance for me. *I never want a boyfriend.*

Katie continues. "Black Hawk left the reservation in Iowa with a thousand women and children. They had to cross the Mississippi River to return to Illinois from Iowa. Black Hawk wanted his people to return to their old hunting grounds and cornfields. His tribe set up camp near the mouth of the Kishwaukee River a few miles from Stillman Creek, not far from Grand Detour. Upon returning, they terrorized the settlers along the Rock River Valley. They killed men, women, and children in their homes. The settlers began making forts, but they weren't fast enough. This led to the fighting of the white man and Indians."

"Didn't the white men have any caves to hide in?" Billie asks.

"Not that I know of. Do you want me to tell you more?"

"Did they scalp any of the white men, Katie?"

"You'll just have to wait and see. Now let me finish my story before I forget it."

"Major Stillman and Bailey, neither of whom had ever seen any fighting, were sent with two battalions of mounted volunteers of 275 men to spy on the Indians. Some mounted volunteer soldiers who had enlisted within the last thirty days and had never seen war, were preparing their evening meal. A group of three Indians were observed coming over the hill by some guards. It was rumored the Indians carried a white-flag to negotiate peace. I also think that some of the soldiers had been drinking.

The soldiers captured the three Indians, taking them prisoner. One of the Indians was shot while trying to escape, the other two got away. Another group of five Indians was sent by Black Hawk to spy on the first group.

When the shooting began and shots could be heard, the second group of Indians retreated back to Black Hawk's camp. A dozen soldiers shot and killed two of the fleeing Indians. When the remainder of the Indians returned to their camp, war hoops were raised. Black Hawk and hundreds of his men rode after the soldiers. The Indians increased their war hoops and rode to meet the terrified white men who retreated to Stillman Run to alarm the other soldiers. Black Hawk's braves were close at their heels. When they returned to camp, Captain Adams tried to reorganize his soldiers who were already retreating.

Eleven soldiers were found dead the following day along with Captain Adams. The Indians had cut some of the soldier's heads, hands and feet off, and they even tore out some of their tongues and hearts. When the bodies were found, there were intestines scattered about the area!"

"Katie, I think that might have been worse than losing your scalp, don't you?"

"Billie, I don't think I would want to die a terrible death like any of those soldiers. Do you know who Abraham Lincoln is?"

"Sure, silly. He was President during the Civil War!"

"He was more than President. He was Captain Abraham Lincoln at the time of the soldiers' deaths. He assisted in the burial of the dead soldiers. The soldiers were the first soldiers to die in the Black Hawk War."

"Katie, can I be Black Hawk today?"

"Sure, you'll make a great Chief Black Hawk, Billie!"

Katie could never say no to poor little Billie. I begin protesting. "That's not fair! I'm always the Indian chief."

"It's not going to kill you to let your brother be the Indian for once. Now scoot before I scalp you all."

We start chasing each other across the warm rocks. It isn't long before I hear Billie, the brave Chief Black Hawk, screaming for help. It takes me a few minutes before I find him. Billie is laying about eight feet down on a four foot wide ledge.

After looking the situation over, I know Billie is in grave danger. "Are you all right?"

Billie begins crying. "No, go for help! I'm afraid to move."

I run to find Katie, Rita, and Bobby. They all are still hiding from each other.

My voice echoes over Castle Rock. "Help! Billie has fallen onto a ledge. I'm serious, guys. This isn't a game. Come on out of hiding. I really need your help."

Katie answers first. "Where are you, Missy?"

"Billie is on a ledge by the big cave!"

After a few minutes, Katie, Rita, and Bobby arrive. I point to the ledge directly below me. "I don't think we can reach him!"

Katie leans over the ledge to get a better view of the situation. "Missy, you're right. There is no way we can help Billie by ourselves."

Being the oldest, Katie takes charge of the situation. She points to a rock a few feet away from the edge of the steep cliffs. "You kids go sit on that rock. I don't need anyone else falling off while I'm in charge. I'm probably in enough trouble already!"

Katie begins pacing. Tears trickle down her cheeks. "This is my fault! I should have been watching all of you better. I need to think for a minute."

Katie gets down on her knees and leans over the cliff. "We need Uncle Frank and Uncle Jimmy to bring some strong ropes to help us get Billie off this darn rock."

She gets up and wipes the sand off her hands as she walks over to me; and then she leans over and whispers in my ear. "Missy, you are the fastest. Run like the devil is chasing you, and get help. If Billie moves an inch in either direction, we just might lose him forever!"

I run as fast as I can; only stopping to put my tennis shoes on when I get to the middle of the rocks.

When I almost reach the bottom of the hill, I slip on some sand and roll the rest of the way down. Out of breath, I get back up on my feet and head for our trailer. Mama is peering out a window looking happy. I sure hope we can save Billie. We have all shed enough tears this last year.

I holler at the top of my lungs. "Mama...Uncle

Frank....Uncle Jimmy...Aunt May...does anyone hear me?"

I open the trailer door and start towards the kitchen where I view Mama in the window. She is in her favorite apron doing what she likes doing best; cooking everyone's lunch.

"Goodness, girl, what are you yelling about? Have you and your sister been fighting again? And how come you're so dirty?"

Mama walks to the front door. "Where are the rest of the kids? It's about time for lunch!"

I try to stop shaking so Mama can understand me. "Uhh...it's Billie. He's fallen off the rocks onto a ledge. Katie's afraid he's going to fall off soon if I don't come with help!"

Uncle Frank and Uncle Jimmy are out checking on their cane poles when they hear me yelling. They both come running in their flip-flops.

"What's wrong? Where are the other kids?" Uncle Jimmy asks me.

Billie's on a ledge about eight feet down from the top of Castle Rock. Katie told me to tell you the ledge is only about four feet wide. We need to bring a strong rope to pull him up. She also said to bring the first aid kit in case he has any injuries she can't see."

Uncle Frank and Uncle Jimmy find a rope that is strong enough to hold Billie. Mama runs to the kitchen to fetch her first aid kit. She always keeps one at the river in case someone gets horned by a fish or has a hook in them.

"Where are the rest of the kids, Missy?" Uncle Jimmy asks.

"They're with Katie. She told them to sit down and not move an inch until help arrives. She is trying to keep Billie calm by telling him stories."

"She should have done that in the first place!" Uncle Jimmy mumbles.

"Do you think you can show us where Billie is?" Uncle Frank asks me.

"I know exactly where they are and how to find the ledge. Our daddy climbed the rocks with us every summer until he died!"

Uncle Frank glares at me. I don't think he likes being reminded Mama was married before.

I hope next summer Mama doesn't have a boyfriend; especially Uncle Frank. *No one can replace Daddy, and I don't want to share my memories of being here with anyone but my family.*

Mama washes her hands and takes off her apron. "What can I do to help?"

"Dot, this is man's work. You just stay here and fix us lunch. I'll bring your boy back." Uncle Frank tells her.

I'm not sure Mama believes him. But I know one thing for sure; she never could climb those rocks.

Tears stream down Mama's cheeks. Aunt May tries consoling her without much luck. *I hope we bring Billie back safe!*

The sun is beating down on us hotter than the devil. Sweat is pouring down Uncle Jimmy's beet red forehead. "You sure we are going in the right direction?"

At this rate, Uncle Jimmy is going to die before we reach Billie. He should have stayed back at the trailer with Mama.

Uncle Frank is in much better shape than I expected him to be. He is keeping up quite well for someone so fat. He is holding on to the rope so tight his fingers are beginning to turn color. I guess he doesn't want to look for the rope if he drops it.

Uncle Jimmy calls out with his voice echoing. "Katie, can you hear me?"

"We're over here, Uncle Jimmy! Can you see us?"

We see Katie waving frantically. I see Rita and Bobby still sitting on the rock far from the ledge. They don't look happy about staying put.

"Over here!" Katie points straight down the side of the cliffs. "Billie is down there on a small ledge!"

When I reach Katie, she leans toward me and whispers. "Thanks for arriving back with help so quick. I don't know how much longer I could have kept Billie awake with my stories about the old West!"

I look down at Billie and pray we aren't too late.

Uncle Frank and Uncle Jimmy tell Katie and me to go sit over on the rock with the other kids. Katie mumbles something about keeping Billie alive up to now. *It's a good thing Uncle Frank doesn't hear her.*

Uncle Frank leans over the ledge to talk to Billie. I can't hear what he says, but he sure looks creepy.

Uncle Frank joins Uncle Jimmy. He has already tied a slip knot on one end of his rope. He throws the other end to Uncle Frank.

Uncle Frank holds the rope in one hand and reaches in his pocket for a handkerchief to wipe the sweat off his face. "Billie, you listen to your Uncle Jimmy. He isn't going to let anything happen to you!"

Uncle Frank takes his end of the rope and ties it to his waist to provide extra protection while he pulls Billie up from the ledge. He walks to the rock we are sitting on and waits for further instructions from Uncle Jimmy.

Uncle Jimmy leans over the edge of the cliff. "Don't reach for the rope until it actually touches you. Then slip it around your waist and hold onto it with all your might. Do you understand me?" He asks.

Billie tells him he understands. Then he says a short prayer out loud asking God to keep him safe along with Uncle Jimmy. We can hear his little voice." If I don't...make...it, Bobby, you can have my baseball bat. And, Missy, you can have all my comic books. Thanks everyone, it has been good knowing you!"

I wipe a tear from my eyes and try my best not to cry and upset Billie. I cross my fingers Billie makes it off the ledge safe.

"Frank, back up and get ready to slowly start pulling!" Uncle Jimmy shouts.

Uncle Jimmy throws the opposite end of the rope to Billie

landing too far from him to reach. After a couple throws, the rope finally lands close enough for Billie to reach.

"Billie, I want you to carefully put the rope over your arms and around your waist," Uncle Jimmy calmly directs. "Now, hold on tight and whatever you do, don't let go. And for Heaven's sake, don't look down! Do you understand me?" Uncle Jimmy asks.

"I...I...understand. I promise not to let go of the rope or look down. Uncle Frank already told me it's a long way to fall and would be a horrible way to die!"

Uncle Jimmy looks in our direction and shrugs his shoulders. Then he gives Uncle Frank a nod to go ahead and pull. He pulls the rope so hard it looks like his eyes are going to pop out of their socket. Every vein on his forehead is sticking out like the edges of the frayed rope he is pulling on. I just know he's going to have a stroke and let go of the rope causing Billie to fall to his death.

I begin praying. "Oh, God, please, please, don't let my little brother die so young!"

After Uncle Jimmy pulls Billie over the ledge, he grabs him tight and brings him to where we are all still sitting. Uncle Frank joins us. Katie sits with her face in her hands; crying like there is no tomorrow. The more we try consoling her, the more she cries. We all tell her it wasn't her fault Billie fell.

Uncle Frank and Uncle Jimmy lead the way back down the rocks. I have never seen them move so fast. They say all the stress and climbing has made them thirsty for a cold beer.

Billie pulls me away from everyone. "Did you notice Uncle Frank was acting strange on top of Castle Rock?" "No, what makes you think he is any different than usual?"

Billie whispers in my ear. "He told me it would be an awful way to die if something happened to the rope. Then he showed me his shiny pocket knife!"

"Are you sure you weren't just hallucinating from the heat? You were on the ledge for a long time."

"I'm sure he showed me his knife and his eyes sort of looked like Dracula's when he's ready to drink your blood!"

"Hmm…there is something strange about him I just can't figure out. *We better keep an eye on him!*"

When we reach the trailer, Mama gives Billie the biggest hug and kiss I ever did see. Billie usually doesn't let Mama give him kisses anymore. He says he is too old for such things. But this time is special; he just holds onto Mama as tight as he can. He tells her that he thought he was never going to see her again.

Later, Katie informs me she didn't think Billie was going to make it off the ledge alive either. She told him stories to comfort both of them.

Chapter Five

It never fails. Every time Mama and Uncle Frank go out to Castle Rock Restaurant and Bar on a Friday or Saturday night, they come home drunk, stumbling, smelling like smoke, and calling each other names.

If I can hear them outside the trailer, the rest of the campers have to hear them. I try covering my head with a pillow but it doesn't help.

"Dot, what were you doing hanging on that man all night long? What, am I not good enough for you? I buy you everything you want!"

Mama has drunk enough by now she isn't frightened of any man. "Why don't you stop being jealous, Frank. Can't I even talk to another man? For crying out loud, I have to talk to men every night when I'm working. If I didn't, I would get fired. And then who would pay the rent and buy groceries? I can't help it if other men think I'm attractive. You thought the same at one time. God gave me this body, and I plan not to let it go to waste!'"

It is wonderful at night when no one is fighting. You can hear the river current flowing over the rocks in the river which is soothing to the soul. The gentle breezes cool my warm moist body from the heat of the day. The crickets rub their legs together to make music, the frogs are croaking, owls hooting, fish gently splash out of the water, and you can hear tree frogs in the distance. It is as if Mother Nature is directing a symphony. It is as God has intended it to be, peaceful and nothing but nature's natural environment without man's interference.

The stars are bright as sparklers all lit up at a Fourth of July picnic. The moon's reflection on the river is breathtaking. I know why Mama feels close to the river. It is a happy, serene place that lets your mind wander so you can imagine you are somewhere different; far from reality.

Morning comes early when you are camping. With the earliest sign of light, everyone is up baiting their fishing poles and checking on their cane poles they left in the water the previous night. You are to be as quiet as a mouse so you don't scare off any fish. I really wonder if fish do have ears. I have never seen any signs of them when Mama chops their heads off and I have to help clean them.

The minute anyone thinks the fish are biting near someone else's fishing line, they quietly reel in their poles and proceed to throw their lines out where the nibble was. The next thing you know, someone is hollering they have a bite. "I've got one...I've got one!" At that precise moment, someone else begins hollering the same thing.

It is a sight to see, grownups excited about a little fish nibbling on their mushy old night crawler. It is even funnier to watch the two fishermen reel in their lines only to find out they have caught each other. You would think they would know enough not to fish so close to each other. Sometimes if you observe adults long enough, you see what you shouldn't do as well as what you should.

At night, just after dark when the dew sets in, we go hunting for night crawlers. Billie holds the flashlight while I try to catch those slimy, cold, dirty, wiggling night crawlers. Billie always loses patience while holding the light for me. He points it to the top of trees and out on the river or in my face. He knows this makes me angry, but he giggles and just keeps on doing it anyway.

Of course, Katie never joins in fishing or catching the bait. She might get her pretty little hands dirty.

"Billie," I whisper, hoping not to scare the night crawlers. "Will you hold the flashlight still? How am I ever going to get enough bait for tomorrow?"

"Okay, but hurry up. I'm tired of holding this light still!" I will have to be quick with my hands before these night crawlers slide right back into their holes. Sometimes as I pull on them, these darn old worms break into two pieces trying to get away.

The ground begins to get damp. We have a coffee can full of worms and Billie can't keep the light from jiggling around any longer.

"Billie, I think we have enough worms for fishing tomorrow, don't you? Let's go get a sweatshirt on and watch Mama fish."

"Okay, but you better watch out for those bats flying above your head or all you are going to be doing is cutting your blonde hair off. And I'm not going to help you!" Billie teases.

We both duck at the same time. Bats start swarming around the trees above our heads. Billie's flashlight shining through the leaves of the trees is causing the bats to swoop down near us. They are getting so close we can almost touch them. I hope none of the bats turn into vampires.

Dracula could be looking for his next victims. Just as we duck again, Billie's flashlight flashes on a big old oak tree nearby. I can see someone behind the tree watching us. Billie drops his flashlight.

"Missy, run. It's Dracula!" Something grabs him before he can get his little feet going.

"I've got you!" Uncle Frank tells Billie, as he holds him up in the air. "You know, Billie, there is more than one way Dracula can drink your blood!" He places Billie back on the ground showing him his knife.

Mama approaches us. "Frank, you stop teasing those kids!

They are already afraid of the dark. And you talking about Dracula is going to give those kids nightmares."

Uncle Frank walks back to the campfire, but not before turning toward us running his fingers down the side of the shiny knife blade.

"Missy, that's the knife he showed me on top of Castle Rock! Do you think he might just use that old knife to kill us?"

"He's just trying to scare us. *And I think it's working.* Just try to forget about him tonight."

We go into the trailer and put on sweatshirts. Then we return back outside to watch Mama fish. Uncle Jimmy has started a nice campfire to keep the dew off of us and help light up the night. I feel safe and warm sitting close to Mama. She will keep an eye on old Uncle Frank.

"Mama, do we have any large marshmallows we can roast?" I ask.

"There is a package on the second shelf of the kitchen cupboard. You and Billie will have to go and find your own sticks to roast them on."

"Billie, there's nothing that tastes as good as roasted marshmallows, don't you agree?"

"Yeah, I like mine warm with no burnt areas. How do you like yours?"

"I like mine real burnt where it almost looks like charcoal."

"That's disgusting, Missy!"

Billie and I sit at the campfire and eat the entire bag of

marshmallows. We are nice and toasty ourselves.

Aunt May always makes Rita and Bobby go to bed early. It is sad they didn't get to join us at the campfire to roast marshmallows. Aunt May says she needs time to herself without kids so she can unwind before she goes to bed. We are only sitting by Mama watching her fish; so why couldn't the twins do the same? They sure do miss out on a lot of fun.

Mama catches four catfish ranging in weight from one to three pounds. Uncle Frank only catches a few small bullheads. He has never been fishing before. Uncle Jimmy catches the granddaddy of all fish; a twenty-five pound catfish on one of his cane poles using chicken livers. That poor fish has chunks out of him everywhere!

"Dot, I've got a big fish on my line this time. It isn't any little bullhead. I can't barely reel it in to shore. It seems like I have been reeling this pole in forever!" Frank says excited.

Mama winks at us. "It's about time you caught a real fish, Frank!"

Uncle Frank keeps reeling his fishing line in until he finally gets his big fish to shore. When he lifts his line out of the water in the dim light, he throws his pole right down at the bank of the river.

"Dot, this isn't any fish. I'm not going to touch the damn thing!" He screams at her.

Mama grabs his pole before the turtle dragged it into the river. Right there in front of all of us was a large snapping turtle. Billie and I sit down on the bank and begin laughing hysterically. We have never seen a grown man throw his fishing pole down before; especially over a little old turtle.

Uncle Frank begins yelling at us. "I don't think this is funny! I'm going to get even with you kids when you least expect it. I'm going to teach you not to laugh at me again. Maybe I'll even tell Dracula where he can find you...alone. And maybe, you'll have an accident just like your daddy—"

"Frank, calm down. For crying out loud, it's just a little turtle and the kids are only teasing you. And don't you ever bring Dan's accident up to me or my kids again. That was uncalled for!"

"I'm sorry, Dot. I was only getting even with your kids for laughing at me and—"

"There's no excuse. I don't ever want you to bring up his name again!"

Uncle Jimmy goes over to Uncle Frank's fishing pole and removes the turtle from the hook. The turtle sure will taste good tomorrow night at our annual fish fry. I doubt Uncle Frank will be cleaning it himself.

Uncle Jimmy always has the best luck fishing. He can catch a fish when no one else is even getting a nibble. He can probably catch a fish in a drought and the river is dry. He is so lucky that way.

Uncle Jimmy, Mama, and Aunt May like to go frogging at night where the creek meets the mouth of the river.

Uncle Frank tells Mama, "Dot, I'm not going to touch no slimy frog let alone eat one of them!"

"Go ahead and be bullheaded, Frank. You can just hold the flashlight for us. No matter what, you're coming with!"

Uncle Frank yells at Mama. "Don't you ever embarrass me in front of another man again!"

Mama gives Uncle Frank a dirty look.

They all grab their nets and off they go with Uncle Frank two steps behind them pouting and mumbling something about how Mama is going to end up like Daddy too, if she doesn't watch it.

Chapter Six

Billie and I wake up early. We don't have to use our old fishing poles today.

"Mama, do we still get to use your fishing poles?" Billie asks.

"I think you two have proved to me you're responsible little fishermen after your last adventure; don't you?"

Uncle Frank put his arm around Billie almost smothering him to death. "I'm going to tie one end of a rope to the dock and the other end to the boat. You will be able to row out a ways on the river and fish all on your own. How's that for being such a big guy?"

"Oh, boy, do you mean it?"

"Sure do! You have to put your life jacket on first."

Billie begins running. "I'll do that right now!"

Mama hands Billie his tackle box and bait. "You can fish out there all day if you want to, but you have to put your own bait on your hook. And there will be no one to fix your line if you lose it."

"I will. I promise!"

"You two need to catch us a lot of fish for tonight's fish fry!" Mama says.

I am sure happy I don't have to bait Billie's fish hook anymore.

Billie is happy as a clam. Mama and Uncle Frank must trust him a lot to let him take out the boat by himself. He will be sure he makes no mistakes while he's in the boat. And maybe one day soon he won't even have to be tied to a rope. Placing the bait on the hook isn't something he's going to like, but he has to do it sometime. No one is going to be around to stop him from reeling his line in when he doesn't get a bite either. If he doesn't catch any fish, he will learn real quick to be patient.

Mama packs Billie a lunch and drink for the day. She makes him his favorite sandwich; bologna and ketchup. She fills a thermos full of fresh lemonade she made this morning. He won't even have to wash his hands before he eats with no adults around. If he really needs to wash, he can just swish his hands in the dirty river water.

I walk over by a big weeping willow tree to fish. There will be plenty of shade and no one else really likes to fish in this spot. I have to be careful, or when I throw my fishing line out, I might catch one of the branches hanging over the river. It is a wonderful spot to read a book when the fish aren't biting, or to just sit and think. I brought along a Bobbsey twins book,

The Secret at the Seashore, which I purchased at a garage sale with money from returning pop bottles. I paid a quarter for the book. It is worth a lot more to me. I won't ever sell it!

I bait my hook with a real juicy night crawler which I put vanilla on. This ought to help me catch a big old catfish, even if it takes awhile in this heat.

I brought along a quilt my Grandma Irene made me to lay on while I read my book. The old quilt has scraps of my old clothes in it. Not that I want to keep my clothes around forever being that most of them were bought at garage sales. Some of them do remind me of happier times when Daddy was still alive. One of the colors I hate the most in my quilt is the brown from my used Brownie outfit. The quilt has a flower sheet on the back with the ugliest colors I have ever seen. Mama gave the sheet to Grandma Irene after Uncle Frank bought her new ones. The thought of him lying on the sheet gives me the creeps.

I read my book for two hours before I finally get a bite on my fishing pole. It jerks so hard it pulls my pole off the fork stick I have it on. This must be the big one. I grab my pole quick. The water is dark, murky, and deep where I'm sitting. I can't swim well either. I jerk my pole and begin reeling in fast.

My line goes slack. *I hope I don't lose my fish.* Right there on top of the water is something swimming towards me and the river bank. It doesn't look too much like any fish I have ever seen. It's long and the sun is shining right off of its back. The closer it gets to me; I can see…its not any fish. It's a snake!

I know poisonous snakes are around the Rock River, but I haven't ever seen one myself before. It sure isn't an old garter snake. Chills are running up and down my spine. My heart is about to leap out of my chest. I touch slimy worms, but there is no way I'm touching any snake if it might be poisonous.

I scream at the top of my lungs. "Help…help…there's a snake!"

I hope my screaming doesn't scare all of Billie's fish away. The closer the snake comes toward the bank, the louder I scream.

Uncle Jimmy and Aunt May are the first to hear my screams. They both come running.

"What's all the screaming about? I can see Billie is fine in his boat. Did you hook yourself?" Uncle Jimmy shouts.

"There's a…a…snake at the end of my fishing line and its coming toward me. I think it's…poisonous!"

"Where is the snake, Missy?"

"There…there's the snake. It's coming toward us!" I yell, as I point to the end of my line. I can just see the top of the snake making ripples in the water as it is swimming directly at me. I think it wants to get even with me for hooking it.

Uncle Jimmy runs for his gun almost tripping on the campfire from last night. It is hard for him sometimes because he has an old injury from when he was in World War II. His run looks more like a fast walk.

Aunt May beats Uncle Jimmy to their trailer. "May, go into the kitchen cupboard and get my 38 as fast as you can!" Uncle Jimmy shouts.

Aunt May rushes into the trailer. They keep their keys on the top shelf of their kitchen cupboards. It is always locked and no one but those two are allowed to touch them. Aunt May brings Uncle Jimmy the pistol, but forgets to retrieve the bullets they keep in a different spot for safety. None of us kids know where the bullets are kept.

"Now go and get the bullets out of the bedroom. I want to get the snake before it comes to shore!"

Aunt May hands Uncle Jimmy the bullets. He runs to the river bank where I am standing and loads his pistol as quick as any cowboy I've ever seen. He fires at the snake and misses. The snake dives under the water as if it anticipates Uncle Jimmy aiming straight at it.

"It's a water moccasin! Missy, move back away from shore. I need to get a better shot at it. I don't want to worry about you getting hurt."

The snake is as angry as an old grizzly bear. It comes right up to the top of the surface and I swear it's looking right at me. That old snake looks like the devil himself. If I were still holding my pole, I would have thrown it in the river; snake and all.

Uncle Jimmy takes aim at the snake again. He doesn't miss this time. He blows him right out of the water. Half of the snake ends up on the river bank right where Uncle Jimmy is shooting. I can't find where the other half ended up.

"Missy, it's a good thing you didn't catch the snake and try to take it off by yourself. You wouldn't be standing here with us right now, darling," Uncle Jimmy informs me.

"What's the matter, Missy? Are you afraid of some little old snake?" Billie yells from the boat. "Uncle Jimmy, you shootin' that old snake out of the water is better than watchin' any old western at the movies. You sure did scatter him all over the bank!" Billie laughs.

Rita and Bobby follow Aunt May out of the trailer. "Yeah, Dad, we didn't know you could shoot like that. It was really cool!" Bobby said grinning from ear to ear.

Mama and Uncle Frank watched Uncle Jimmy blow up the snake, too. At least the world will be rid of one more snake. Katie peeks out of the trailer window at me. *Being a bit of a snake herself; she probably wanted me to get bit.*

Chapter Seven

Billie and I continue to fish for a couple more hours. The thought of that old snake still gives me chills. *I know one thing for sure; I am never going to use vanilla again.*

Mama yells halfway across the river. "Billie, it's time for you to bring the boat in and clean up. You get to help us clean your fish for supper!"

You can see his silly little grin from the bank where I am standing. It isn't taking Billie long to get his boat in. He sure wants to clean his own fish. If you are going to be a fisherman, Mama says you have to clean your own fish.

"Mama, I want to take my own fish guts out. Can I scale my own bluegill, too?"

"You have been such a good little fisherman; I will show you how to scale your fish today."

"Mama, I think I love the taste of bluegill the best. But those darn boogers swallow the hook every time. I had to cut my line and put a new hook and sinker on every time."

"I'm so proud of you, Billie. I think you will be as good of a fisherman as I am someday!"

Mama lets Billie scale his bluegill. She cuts their heads off and slits their stomachs so Billie can take the guts out. Some fish have to be scaled and others have to be skinned. *I would rather scale a fish than skin it.*

Uncle Jimmy gets the turtles out of a separate box tied to the dock. I'm sure glad I don't have to help clean them. Uncle Jimmy takes it upon himself to clean the turtles. It is more work explaining the cleaning process to someone and he doesn't want anyone to waste the meat.

I would have wanted to let those darn turtles loose if they didn't taste so good. Some parts taste like chicken, some taste like steak. They are sure good. The turtle shells are pretty, especially the painted turtle shells. Uncle Jimmy nails them to a tree for everyone to see.

"Everyone who caught a fish, come on over to the table. You have to clean your share. This includes you, Frank!" Mama says, winking at him.

The table we're cleaning on looks more like a kitchen counter than any old fish table I have ever seen. It even has a marble counter with a hand pump and sink to rinse the fish off. The table is so tall everyone has to stand up to use it.

Mama winks at Bobby. "Your job is to skin the fish. I am designating you to teach Frank so he can assist you." From the look on Bobby's face, I think he would rather skin them all himself. Uncle Frank is taking more meat off than skin. He seems to be a bit too happy with using the fillet knife.

"Billie and Rita, you can take the guts out of the fish. If you find any eggs, there is a separate bowl on the table to place them in," Mama directs.

Aunt May walks over to Rita and Bobby. "You better do a good job. Your dad won't be happy if you throw away his fish eggs."

Uncle Jimmy always did say those fish eggs are as good as any caviar he has ever tasted.

"Missy, you can help me crack the fish over the heads with the hammer. You better make sure you pay attention to how I do it. We don't want to make the fish suffer!" Mama says.

Uncle Frank grabs the hammer. "Let me take a crack at killing those fish!"

"I don't mind you helping with the killing of these fish, Frank, but pay attention to how I kill them. I don't need you wasting anymore of the meat!"

She cuts a section off the cheeks of the fish after she cleans them. This is supposed to be the filet. It is her favorite part.

Aunt May's job is to supervise everyone. She really doesn't like cleaning fish much being she is the oldest of eight children, and the main protein growing up was fish.

Mama and Aunt May are going to cook the fish in a secret beer batter recipe they never give out. It was passed down to them from their grandma and they are going to pass it down to us girls when we are old enough not to tell the secret ingredients.

Mama sets two large gallon jugs out in the sun with water and tea bags. All of the kids are going to drink homemade sun tea and lemonade made from freshly squeezed lemons. The adults are going to get a head start on drinking beer for going out later tonight. They won't have to spend as much money on beer when the band starts at Castle Rock Bar. Once the band begins, the price of drinks goes up.

Aunt May and Mama have several cast-iron pans already heating up on our campfire. They are going to cook about fifteen catfish, bullheads, and Billie's bluegill. Mama has one special pan ready to cook the frog legs in. Uncle Jimmy has his pan ready for the turtles. "Mama, I love watching you cook those frog legs. I sure can't wait to eat one!" I say, with my mouth already starting to water.

Those frog legs just keep jumping in the pan even without their bodies. Once, a leg jumped right out of the pan onto Mama's kitchen floor. It almost scared poor Mama half-to-death. I couldn't stop laughing at Mama. She usually isn't frightened of anything.

"Frank, I'm giving you the corn duty. All you have to do is husk the corn over in the barrel, and place the ears in the large corn boiler over the fire," Mama directs him.

Uncle Frank reaches into a cooler. "You're giving me the hottest job here. I'll need another beer first. In fact, I think I'll just keep the cooler close to me!"

Cooking is an all day event when we have our family fish fry. Everyone is expected to pitch in and do the work. Everyone except Katie, she doesn't ever help clean any of the fish, turtles, or frogs.

Earlier today Aunt May and Mama prepared homemade potato salad, macaroni salad, and baked beans. They just sat in the trailer visiting, laughing, and cooking more like two best friends than sisters. They are proud of their cooking skills and rightfully so. They are the best cooks I know, and most restaurants want to hire Mama as their cook.

Oh...those fish taste so good. They are crispy on the outside and flaky in the middle. There isn't any fish smell or grease dripping off of any of the fish cooked. The tails are nice and crisp. But oh...the tail; it is the best part of the fish!

"If anyone doesn't want their fish tail, I'll eat it!" I yell. No one answers me. I guess they all seem to like the tails as much as I do.

"Mama, can you pass me a frog leg please?" I never get to eat very many frog legs; there usually isn't enough for us kids. I like catfish and turtle the best anyway.

"Dot, can you pass me another bullhead?"

"Sure, Frank, but don't you want to try some of the turtle?"

"One of the turtles was chomping on Billie's foot. I'm not eating anything that had a muddy shoe in its mouth!"

"Frank, why does it matter? You don't eat the mouth,"

Mama says laughing. Everyone else at the table laughs at Mama too, including old Uncle Frank.

Katie refuses to eat fish, and she certainly isn't going to try the turtle or frog legs. She says she isn't about to eat anything that eats worms. She loves Mama's potato salad the best. She ate at least four helpings. She should have eaten more baked beans, and then she won't mind sleeping in the same bedroom with me later. I eat at least three helpings of the beans. Later I plan on eating more if there is any left. I sure do love these beans, but they sure don't like me. I almost feel sorry for Katie having to share the bedroom.

Chapter Eight

Aunt May hollers to us kids. "You can do the dishes and clean the mess up from dinner while we're gone. It will keep you out of trouble!"

"Aunt May… Mama, Katie didn't clean any of the fish. She didn't even catch any. She should do the dishes and clean up everything by herself. It's not fair!" I protest, as I stomp my feet.

"Mama, you know I don't eat fish! It makes me sick to even look at one, let alone eat it," Katie whines.

"We're going to get cleaned up to go out. We don't want to hear another word out of you kids," Aunt May says, with Mama in agreement.

The adults are all going to go dancing at Castle Rock. How anyone can walk, let alone go dancing after eating all this food, is beyond me. I can hardly move. It hurts to even do the dishes.

"After you're through cleaning up, you kids can play games.

We want you in bed by ten," Mama says.

"Billie...Rita, I want you in your own trailer and in bed by ten. Just be glad you're getting to stay out late. I don't want any excuses later on!" Aunt May hollers.

At least Rita and Bobby will get to stay up later than eight and we will have someone to play with. Uncle Jimmy and Aunt May must have figured they would sneak out anyway while they are at the bar and no one is watching them.

Mama puts on a white dress with black polka dots on it. It has black netting under the skirt which makes it flare out from the waist down. It really shows off her figure. She has curled her hair in bobby pins; making real tight curls all over her head. She has a black silk scarf around her neck. Then she puts silver and black clip-on earrings on, and places her new black patent leather shoes with tall skinny heels and pointy toes on her feet. Mama sort of reminds me of Lucille Ball. I don't know how she is going to dance in those shoes. They make her look like she only has three toes.

"You look real pretty tonight, Mama," Katie remarks.

"Thank you for the compliment. You make sure those kids mind you tonight. I don't want to come home and hear about any fighting!"

"I promise! You don't have to worry about us."

Katie doesn't listen. She goes four trailers down from ours to visit a boy about the same age as she is. His parents aren't home either. In fact, most of the adults aren't home if they are still able to dance. They are all up at Castle Rock dancing.

"Missy, can we catch fireflies instead of playing games?" Bobby asks.

"What do you think, Rita?" I ask.

"Well, my mom has some empty jars with lids on them in the trailer. I suppose we can use them. We can poke holes in the lids so the fireflies stay alive."

"We can make rings out of some of them?" Rita suggests

"Sure, I like watching them glow on my fingers."

We tie long grass around our fingers and squish the bottom of the fireflies onto the top of our fingers. Billie and Bobby just like to take the fireflies apart and put the bottoms in their hair. *I hope I use the brush before he does in the morning.*

We can hear music and laughter coming from the trailer Katie is in. It sure is getting loud in there.

"Missy, can we peek in the trailer window to see what Katie's laughing about?" Billie asks, with a devilish grin on his face.

"Yeah, can we sneak up on her and peek through the window?" Rita and Bobby chime in.

"I guess, but I don't think any of you know how to sneak up on anyone. You better promise me you'll be real quiet!"

"We will, we promise," they whisper loudly.

As we approach the window, Bobby trips on a minnow bucket someone left out in front of the trailer window. It makes such a loud racket; we all take off in different directions and hide.

We can see Katie opening up the trailer's front door. She must have heard Bobby trip over the bucket.

"If you kids are out there, I'm going to get even with you!" She hollers.

Giggling can be heard from different directions, but no one can be seen. We all hide pretty well.

I guess Katie being in the old trailer is more fun than her being out here bossing us all around. *I wish I had a camera to take a photo of Katie babysitting. Then Mama would know she doesn't pay attention to us when boys are around.*

After a while, we get some of Grandma Irene's quilts out to lie on. We all lay on our backs and watch the stars.

"Does anyone want to see who can count the most stars?" Rita asks.

Everyone pipes up. "I do…I do…."

The stars are brighter at Castle Rock. There aren't many houses around and the nearest town is about five or six miles away.

"I bet I can count the most!" Rita boasts.

"You probably can't count to fifty," Bobby says teasing her.

"We'll just have to see."

I lose count at about one hundred stars; I can't remember which stars I already counted and which ones I haven't.

Billie looses count after about thirty. Rita counts over 100, but she can't keep track of which stars she already counted either.

"I counted at least 125 stars!" Bobby brags.

"I thought you were going to beat me, Rita."

"I lost track and got bored. You just didn't have anything better to think about, Bobby."

We all agree Bobby won the contest. He counted 125 stars.

"Let's see how many constellations we can find," Bobby suggests.

"I think I can beat you on how many constellations you can find, Bobby," Rita boasts again.

"I don't want to do a contest. I don't know many constellations; I couldn't even count many stars," Billie whines.

We decide to find the constellations as a group, just for fun. The first one we find is the Big Dipper, then we find the Little Dipper, Orion, Seven Sisters, Leo, Hercules, Little Bear, Sagittarius, and Rita finds the Gemini Twins at the same time as Bobby, it figures; with them being twins themselves.

We lose track of time and decide it must be getting close to ten. We all say goodnight and go into our trailers.

Not long after Billie and I go into the trailer, Katie comes home. Her face seems to be bright red, and her hair is messed up. She says she is going to get ready for bed and we had better do the same. Too bad she came back home before Mama. .It would have been nice to see someone yell at her and boss her around. *I will get even—I ate beans.*

Something wakes me up about midnight. I can hear loud voices coming from the campfire which is now roaring. I can vaguely make out some of the shadows distorted by the flickering of the flames.

People are stumbling, laughing, and I even think I hear someone crying. Aunt May always cries over her babies growing up every time she gets drunk. Mama usually is a happy drunk at first, but the longer the night goes on, the more she drinks, then you better watch out.

Uncle Jimmy always places his arm around everyone's neck; hanging on for dear life. When my Step-Grandpa Roy is around, the men better watch out. He kisses on their women and smacks their butts. This usually starts fights with Grandma Irene and the men. I hope Grandma Irene and Step-Grandpa Roy don't stay at our trailer tonight. I don't like Step-Grandpa Roy much better than Uncle Sammy or Uncle Frank.

Step-Grandpa Roy told all us kids, "I'm not your Grandpa. You brats better just call me Roy. I've got my own grandchildren and I sure in the hell don't need more!"

Maybe this is why he tries brushing up against all the women's breasts and us girls; including my little budding blossoms.

If I'm lucky, maybe they will stumble into the river and sober up. No such luck tonight! They are getting louder and drunker. This is going to be one long, sleepless night. I wonder if Katie and Billie are awake and can hear everything. Katie sure looks like she's asleep. Usually nothing wakes her.

I don't know how they can't hear everything all these adults are screaming at Castle Rock Restaurant and Bar. I swear every once in a while I can hear echoes. I hear Uncle Frank suggest they all pick teams for a volleyball game. This I have to see for myself! From my view, they can't even walk, let alone play volleyball.

I crawl to the living room picture window, bend down low, and watch what they call volleyball. It should be named jolly-ball because everyone is too busy laughing to even volley. Mama trips on her heel and dives head first into the dirt with Uncle Jimmy landing right on top of her. She is laughing so hard it seems to be catchy. Uncle Jimmy piles on top of Mama, Aunt May piles on top of Uncle Jimmy, and the pile continues until they all look like bowling pins which have just been struck with a sixteen pound bowling ball.

Everyone continues laughing until I hear someone yell, "Get the hell off of me. You're killing me. I can't breathe!" I hear the sentence repeated louder and louder until it is a scream.

Mama is at the bottom of the very large pile; all dirty, hair a mess and the bottom of her dress is torn off. All Mama is wearing is the top of her dress and her underwear. With one shiny, black leather, very pointy high heel shoe in hand; she emerges. She begins beating anyone close with the bottom of her high heel. You can hear screams coming from everyone in her path.

I hear someone scream, "No more! Ow! No more! That hurts, let me up!"

Everyone begins scrambling out of Mama's path.

"Stop Dot, you're killing me. That heel is sharp. Ow!"

Mama must have regained her senses; she finally puts the shoe down. Everyone resumes laughing again. She has rescued the rest of her dress and wraps it around her tiny waist. They all end up around the campfire resuming their drinking; even Mama, without her very pointy shoes this time.

Not long after the laughter stops, I hear a smack; followed by Mama's very loud voice. "Frank, if you think I'm not going to talk to Roger or any other men, you are highly mistaken. Stop being so jealous, it's not very becoming. If you don't like it, you can leave anytime!"

Yes! It is about time she tells old Uncle Frank to leave.

Aunt May, Uncle Jimmy, Grandma Irene, and Roy, retreat to my aunt and uncle's very small trailer. Everyone else also retreats to their trailers. The only two left at the very bright campfire are Uncle Frank and Mama.

Mama isn't going to let anyone push her around. She has taken care of herself since she was fifteen and is a very independent woman. She loves to be around people.

Mama and Uncle Frank head for our trailer screaming at each other the entire way. I crawl back to my bedroom before I get caught watching them. It's just like watching a soap opera. If I get caught, Mama's anger might just be directed at me instead of Uncle Frank!

Their anger heats up as they enter our trailer. There is no way

I'm not going to escape hearing every word they say. I don't know how Billie and Katie can sleep.

"Dot, I'll kill you if I catch you with another man!"

"You don't need to worry about that. After being around you, you ruined it for me. I can barely look at another man without wanting to vomit. And I'd like to see you try it!"

"All you women are tramps; this includes those two daughters of yours. Just look at Katie kissing them boys while she is supposed to be babysitting. I don't know what I ever saw in you!"

"If you want to live one more day, Frank, you'll never talk about my girls like that again!"

I know Mama means every word of what she is saying to Uncle Frank, drunk or not. *I'd like to pop him myself for calling us girls' names.*

"Dot, you don't have to worry about me. I'm leaving!"

"You fool! You're too drunk to walk let alone drive. You might just get yourself killed if you don't kill someone else first."

"You could only be so lucky. But maybe—never mind."

Uncle Frank slams the trailer door with Mama continuing to yell until she is hoarse. She finally gives up on him coming back and stumbles into her bedroom. I sure hope old Uncle Frank gets lost driving home drunk and can't find his way back to our house or this trailer.

We will have to be extra quiet in the morning with Mama having a hangover and being mad at Uncle Frank. I brought a deck of cards to bed to play solitaire after I finish my Bobbsey Twins book. Katie and I can play rummy quietly if she wakes up before noon. Billie will read his comic books or play with his army men until we are told we can get up. Maybe if we are lucky, there will be a cool breeze blowing in our small bedroom window. Sleeping is much easier if it isn't so hot and old Uncle Frank isn't around to argue with Mama.

We will have a lot of work to do when the adults finally do get out of bed. We have to clean the trailer, put everything away by the river, make sure we leave the campfire safe, and pack our belongings. Uncle Frank conveniently won't have to help with him gone now.

No one mentions old Uncle Frank's name or the fight. Aunt May and Uncle Jimmy offer us a ride home. Everyone quietly does their chores. I am glad it is peaceful! I want to hear the flowing of the river current one last time.

Chapter Nine

When we arrive home, Uncle Sammy is glad to see everyone. A wink is given in my direction as he smacks my butt. He tries getting close to Katie. She immediately drops the cast-iron pan she is carrying so she can bend down to pick it up just as he approaches her. The pan dropping makes a lot of noise. Mama looks in Uncle Sammy's direction. He gets the hint and walks to another room.

Sandy is sure glad to see us. She doesn't like being left behind with Uncle Sammy. He hates animals and doesn't give her any attention. With her tail wagging a mile-a-minute she gives everyone kisses.

Mama doesn't say much to old Uncle Frank. Unfortunately for us, he arrived home the night before. It looks like he didn't get much sleep. His eyes have dark circles under them and they are bloodshot. He is still wearing the same clothes, and he reeks of beer and cigarettes. *I don't want my clothes smelling like some dead animal. I stay far away from him.*

Katie is still grounded. She stays in the yard and sunbathes in pink shorts and a pink sleeveless top. Our yard is huge; there are a lot of bushes close to our house so no one can see her. We have pear trees, apple trees and a few cherry trees by our barn. Mama has plenty of room for flower gardens, a vegetable garden, and even a compost heap. The compost heap comes in handy to fertilize all Mama's gardens. She cans everything she grows. Fresh canned goods always taste better than store bought, and she sure has enough room in her walk-in pantry to store food. We have several jars of canned fruit, applesauce and vegetables left from last year. But we are out of Mama's good pickles and canned salmon.

Every year Mama goes fishing in Wisconsin for salmon with Aunt May and Uncle Jimmy. She usually catches at least one salmon weighing twenty-five to thirty-five pounds. She keeps the dead fish in a cooler packed in ice until she arrives back home to clean, cook, and can the salmon. Aunt May and Mama can the salmon together and share the canned jars between them.

The canned salmon makes the best salmon patties in the world. It is a good thing they know how to fish; it saves a lot of money. Canned salmon is pretty expensive and more money than Mama can spare with her budget. I can't figure out how a petite woman can catch such large fish. Mama says it takes her almost an hour to land her salmon, but it is worth every minute.

It is too hot to even sit at the kitchen table to eat when Mama does her canning. She tries to do her canning late at night or early in the morning when she isn't working. This is when our kitchen is the coolest.

We have a couple large oak trees that give us shade early in the morning. Mama brings her fan in the kitchen from her bedroom. She opens all the windows, closes the curtains, turns the radio on, and sings country western songs as she cans. She seems perfectly happy in the steaming hot kitchen. Sweat just pours off me. I feel like I'm going to faint.

"Billie, can you go pick me some cucumbers for pickles?" Mama asks.

"Sure, I'm hungry for your fresh pickles, Mama."

Mama prepares her pots and jars for canning. Then she gets the cucumbers ready. *I can't wait to eat those pickles.*

I don't know how Mama does it. Standing in the hot kitchen all day over the stove is more than I can handle and she has a hangover.

"You know, Mama. You should sell your pickles at the store. They are the best pickles around!" I say as she places them in the jars.

"Thank you, Missy. You saying that makes all the work worth it. You guys are so sweet I am going to make us a pie for dessert tonight. Missy, go in the pantry and get me a couple jars of my canned apples."

I can't wait for the pie to be done.

Mama starts singing along with the radio in the kitchen. I

don't know how she can be happy after fighting the night before. But I'm sure glad she is in a baking mood.

"Mama, you make the best pies I have ever tasted."

The smile on Mama's face almost makes my heart melt like fudge on ice cream. Nothing makes her more proud than people loving her cooking and baking.

The smile doesn't last long. The local news broadcast comes on the radio.

"Early this morning, Roger Miller of Dixon, Illinois swerved to miss what the police think was a deer on Il Route 2 near Castle Rock. Miller's car ended up upside down in the Rock River trapping him. Friends state they were out dancing and drinking with Miller until about one at Castle Rock Restaurant and Bar. There are no other injuries reported. Stay tuned for your local weather...."

Mama sits down at the kitchen table. Tears stream down her cheeks. *It breaks my heart to watch her cry.*

Old Uncle Frank puts his hand on Mama's shoulder. "Dot, I'm sorry about Roger."

Mama pushes his hand away. "Don't you ever pretend you cared about Roger! You threatened to kill him yourself. Where were you after you left the trailer?"

"You heard the radio. Roger had an accident. Dot, you really don't think I'm capable of killing someone?"

"I'm sorry. I'm just upset. Roger was really a gentle man. I know you didn't—I can't talk about this right now. This is too much for me to take in!"

Mama turns off the radio and continues working on the pie crust. Every now and then I can see her wiping the tears slowly falling onto her cheeks. I think her hearing about Roger's accident brings back memories of Daddy dying. It sure does for me. I head to my bedroom and bury my head in my pillow; crying myself to sleep.

Uncle Sammy is really getting on everyone's nerves. He doesn't do anything around the house but make a mess. It seems like Katie and I are always cleaning up after him. He helps himself to all our food without even asking Mama. She'll go in the refrigerator to get carrots for a roast and they are all gone. At first she thinks us kids are taking everything. Mama even grounds us for a day because she thinks we lied to her. The last straw is when she goes into the refrigerator to get a couple of eggs to make a meatloaf and there is none. She knows she still had eggs left earlier in the day. The farmer down the road just brought her some of his beautiful brown eggs from his prize chickens.

"Frank, Sammy, Katie, Billie, Missy, come here. I want to know who ate the last of my eggs. And I want to know the truth!"

I think she knows we kids didn't eat her eggs. I am the only one who ever eats eggs, and I don't know how to cook them. Uncle Frank is too lazy to cook eggs even if he did know how to cook. The only person left is Uncle Sammy.

"Sam, did you eat my eggs?" Mama asks him. "I need those

eggs to make a meatloaf for supper. I told you to ask before you take anything. One more time and you either find a new place to live or you purchase your own groceries! Do you hear me, Sam?"

"I'm sorry. I won't take anything again without asking first. I promise! Do you want me to go to the farmer and see if he has any eggs left?" Uncle Sammy asks.

"No, you can just eat hamburgers now. I'm not in the mood to cook a big meal any longer!" Mama says angrily.

I sure am glad Uncle Sammy got caught taking the last of Mama's eggs. It serves him right for all the times he got us kids in trouble. Besides, I hate meatloaf. I got sick the last time I ate it and threw up all night. I probably had the flu since no one else got sick. I don't care if I ever eat meatloaf again or even smell it cooking. Everyone else loves Mama's meatloaf.

It's too bad Mama doesn't kick Uncle Sammy out. What is it going to take for her to see what a creep he can be? I will make it my business to keep my eye on him and tell Mama everything he does wrong.

I never knew a hamburger could taste so good. Every time I look across our kitchen table at Uncle Sammy my hamburger tastes better and better. We don't have hamburgers very often so they are always a treat. Mama spreads butter lightly on the bottom of our hamburger buns, toasts them to perfection, and then she put the buns on the skillet lid to steam. She adds a small amount of cold water to the ground beef to make them fluffy, puts a small pat of butter in the middle of each hamburger patty pressing them gently so the meat doesn't get tough. And then she cooks them till there is just a little pink left in the middle. I have never tasted any other burger as good as Mama's. We call them "Mama's Better Butter Burgers."

Mama and Uncle Frank go out for a drive in the country after supper. They want a little time by themselves. I think they want to discuss Roger's dying. They aren't going to get any alone time around here. Mama tells us to do the dishes and clean up the kitchen while she is gone. This leaves Katie and me alone with Uncle Sammy. Billie is outside playing with his army men with Sandy by his side. Uncle Sammy is just sitting at the kitchen table watching us while we clean and do the dishes. Katie and I don't say a word to each other while we do them. *I wonder what Uncle Sammy is up to next.*

Uncle Sammy just sits at the table guzzling his beer. His eyes are glazed over like Norman Bates in *Psycho*. He has an alarming smirk on his face. He looks like he is a bit psycho himself.

Without any warning he gets up from his chair and turns Mama's radio on really loud. There is a Ray Charles song playing on the radio. I usually love to hear him sing, but not today with old Uncle Sammy lurking about.

He begins singing along with the radio as he grabs our broom to dance with.

"You girls want to dance?" he asks. "Come on, you know you want to dance with me. No one's around. What are you afraid of? Your old Uncle Sammy hasn't ever hurt you, now has he? Let me show you how a real man dances. I can show you how to move those hips. Who wants to go first?"

Katie calmly says, "Uncle Sammy, you know we have to finish doing these dishes and clean the kitchen before Mama comes home. Why don't you wait for Mama and maybe she'll dance with you?"

As I reach for a dry dishtowel in a cupboard across the kitchen, Uncle Sammy drops the broom and grabs me.

"Dance with me. Show Katie you aren't afraid to dance with a real man!"

"Uncle Sammy, I don't like dancing with anyone. In fact, I don't like to dance at all! Besides, I need to finish the dishes before Mama and Uncle Frank return home."

"Come on, Missy, this is no way to be to your Uncle Sammy. Didn't you miss me just a little bit?" Uncle Sammy quickly grabs me, swinging me around to face him. "Just put your right arm around my waist, then put your left hand on my shoulder and follow my moves."

Katie shouts. "Uncle Sammy, stop! Let, Missy go! Please. She's too young to dance like that. You don't know what you're doing. Let go of her now!"

I sure hope Mama returns home soon. Uncle Sammy smells like a brewery. He must have been drinking all day. He is really making me nervous.

"Katie, are you getting jealous of Missy now? You want me to show you how to dance? Come on, I bet you've never had a real man show you how to dance, have you? Those little boys you play with won't know what to do with you if you even give them a chance. You know you want a little kiss from your Uncle Sammy. Let me show you how a real man kisses, honey. It won't be a peck like your little boyfriend Charlie gives you. A kiss from me will make your knees go weak!"

Uncle Sammy lets me go so fast I almost fall flat on my face onto the kitchen floor. Katie looks frightened. We have never seen Uncle Sammy look like this before. Katie backs up as far as she can go as Uncle Sammy places his hands on both sides of her face. He has her pinned up against the pantry door with nowhere to escape. I can see beads of sweat on poor Katie's frightened face.

"Come on, Katie, just one little dance with your old Uncle Sammy. Don't tell me you don't like to dance. I bet you dance with Charlie. I bet he hasn't even kissed you with his tongue in your mouth. I'll do all that and more! I'll even show you how to move your hips to the music really nice and slow."

"Uncle Sammy, please let me go? You don't know what you're doing. Mama's going to be home real soon. Please stop!" she cries.

"I have been watching you every day, Katie. You know you want me. I can see it in your eyes. The wait will have been worth it; you'll see!"

Uncle Sammy puts his arms around Katie real tight and moves her body with his. He is holding her so close you can't get a pin between them. It looks like he is going to smother

her. Katie is trying frantically to push him away. But he is too strong and she can't budge him.

"Doesn't this feel real nice? Oh…Katie…this feels so…good. Doesn't it make you want more, Katie? How about a kiss for your favorite uncle?"

I pound on Uncle Sammy's back. "Stop! Leave my sister alone! You're hurting her!"

"Go away, Missy. I don't want to hurt you!" Uncle Sammy shouts. He pushes me away with one hand while he continues hanging onto Katie with his other.

Uncle Sammy grabs Katie's face and pulls it toward him. I can smell his breath from where I am standing and it makes me want to puke. His face looks like he hasn't shaved for a couple of days so his stubble is rubbing on Katie's poor flawless face causing it to become red.

Katie gags. Uncle Sammy's whole mouth covers hers. I see fear in her eyes as she struggles to get free.

I need to help her and fast. I'm afraid of what Uncle Sammy might do to her next. I wish Mama was still here. She would let Uncle Sammy have it.

I take a very large cast-iron skillet out of the dish drain and swing it with all my might at the back of Uncle Sammy's legs. He lets go of Katie and falls to the floor moaning. It serves him right. *I hope I broke his leg and he can't run after me.*

Uncle Frank and Mama walk into the kitchen as the cast-iron skillet lands on Uncle Sammy's legs. Mama looks shocked at the scene she just witnessed. *My aim isn't as good as I would like it to have been if Uncle Sammy had been facing in my direction. I would have aimed at his third leg, and he would never have thoughts like that again.*

Mama's face turns as red as her freshly polished nails. She screams at Uncle Sammy. "Go to your room! Frank and I will be there in a few minutes to talk to you! Don't you even think of leaving this house until I'm done talking to you!"

She asks us if we are all right and if Uncle Sammy hurt us in any way. Katie and I know what she means and we both assure her he hadn't.

Mama tells us to finish our dishes and go take a nice hot bubble bath. I think she knows we both want Uncle Sammy's sweaty, smoky, beer breath off of us. He made us feel dirty.

"Girls, if you want to talk later, just tell me."

Uncle Sammy is standing in the living room glaring at me. He should have listened to Mama. He is going to be in big trouble with her now.

"Sam, if those girls tell me you put a hand on them, I'm calling the police to have you arrested. You make me sick to my stomach. Pack your bags! I'm giving you fifteen minutes to get out of my house, out of my sight, and as far away from my kids as you can possibly go! If any of your items get left behind, I will have Frank drop them off at whatever poor soul's door you end up at! And, Sam, don't ever come on my property again!" Mama screams.

"Dot, I am truly sorry, I didn't know what I was doing. I am drunk and—"

"And what? You grabbed another beer? Stop making excuses. There's nothing you can say to me or my kids to make things better."

Uncle Frank doesn't say anything to Uncle Sammy. He just follows Mama around looking stunned. I think he is afraid Mama is going to throw him out next. If it was up to me, I would kick him out immediately. *He frightens me.*

Uncle Frank helps Uncle Sammy pack and carry his belongings to his car. It looks like they are having a serious talk out by his car. I try listening through the kitchen window. I think I hear Uncle Frank tell Uncle Sammy it's too bad they came back so early. But I must have misunderstood. They both start laughing. And then I hear Roger's and Daddy's names. I bet Mama wouldn't find them laughing about Daddy so funny.

When they finish talking, Uncle Frank gives Uncle Sammy one last pat on the back. If it were me, I would have given him one last smack upside his head.

Chapter Ten

It has been a couple of weeks since Uncle Sammy moved out. Mama tells us we are going to turn the guest room into a study. We don't have enough books to call it a library.

Mama is going to paint the study a crimson red, being red is her favorite color. She purchased an old lace tablecloth at a garage sale which only has one small stain on it at the very edge. She cut the stain off and made lace curtains for the window.

The floors are hardwood, and the trim is all natural. Mama purchased an oriental rug from a garage sale last summer. The rug has some crimson in it which matches our freshly painted walls. The rug is going to look great in our study.

Mama takes us around to a few garage sales to find more furnishings and books for our new room. We find two green marble floor lamps real cheap. The lamps will give us more light in the room to read by. I find a complete set of Franklin W. Dixon, Hardy Boy books at one garage sale for barely anything. I also found a few Bobbsey Twins books at another garage sale. It feels like Christmas and my birthday combined. We usually only receive a couple presents for Christmas. I even found an Amelia Earhart novel I wanted to read in the school library but it was always checked out. Billie found some army men at a garage sale which Mama purchased for him. He really doesn't care for reading anything but comic books. Katie won't be caught dead at a garage sale so she stayed home and listened to the radio.

We go to a church rummage sale and find two red over-stuffed arm chairs which almost match the one we have in our living room. The arms are a little worn, but Mama can get Aunt May to crochet some arm chair covers to cover up the thin spots.

Mama finds a real nice man who works at the church sale to deliver the chairs to our home free of charge. The church even gives us a couple of bookshelves for free that didn't sell earlier in the day. *It must be our lucky day.*

Uncle Frank helps Mama arrange the furniture in our new study. Mama even gives me two whole shelves for all of my new books. They look nice on those shelves instead of being in a box in the back of my closet. Our new study looks like a picture in a magazine!

Mama and Uncle Frank are going out to dinner at the Castle Rock Restaurant and Bar for their Friday night fish fry. Of course, the fish won't taste as good as Mama's. We kids can't wait. Katie and I don't have to worry about old Uncle Sammy bothering us anymore. It has been a while since we have been home alone without any adults to supervise us.

We make bologna and potato chip sandwiches for supper. Billie puts ketchup on his bologna sandwich and I put mustard on mine. Katie puts potato chips, onion slices, and mustard on hers. After we put our sandwich together, we smash it to make the potato chips stay between the slices of bread. The crunchiness and tartness of my sandwich makes it taste good. We open a jar of Mama's homemade dill pickles and a jar of her pickled beets to go along with our sandwiches. Our meal is such a special treat after all the fancy meals Mama makes for Uncle Frank and Uncle Sammy. And no one can make better beets than Mama.

There is a mom and pop grocery store a few blocks away called Candy's General Store. They have the best penny candy you can get your hands on. They have rock candy, candy cigarettes, jaw breakers, licorice, Bazooka bubble gum, and wax bottles with liquid in them. They also have every type of comic book a boy could ever want. For 12 cents Billie can purchase *DC* or *Marvel* comic books. *I don't see what's so great about those comic books, but they sure make Billie happy.* It takes him a half hour to choose one. He chose *Marvel's Strange Tales* for 12 cents. It is going to be Dr. Strange's first appearance.

After supper, we take a walk to Candy's General Store. Mama gives us each a quarter to spend. Billie says he is going to buy two comic books, I am going to purchase a lot of penny candy, and Katie is going to look at the newest teen magazines to see if she has enough money to purchase one. We all feel rich.

When we return home, we decide to work on a 1000 piece puzzle for a while. I share my candy, and we talk about how nice it is not to have Uncle Sammy around. Billie says he misses beating Uncle Sammy at checkers.

"Katie, can we make prank phone calls to people like we used to when Mama was gone?" Billie asks.

"I'll think about it. If you tell Mama she will ground me again!"

"Please? We won't tell. We promise!" Billie and I try to convince her.

"Okay, but let's wait until dark. It's more fun then," Katie says chuckling.

We work on a beautiful puzzle of mountains, flowers, and a lake. It might take a while to finish. I share my cigarette candy with Katie and Billie. We pretend to be Mama when she smokes. She always makes sure she holds her cigarette in her hand so you can see how beautiful her fingernails look. I pretend to be Uncle Frank ready to light her cigarette. Billie even tries walking like Mama while he smokes his candy cigarette. Billie would have made a cuter girl than a boy.

Last Halloween, Mama put a dress, high heels, and a scarf on Billie. She even put lipstick on him. Everyone thought

Billie was the cutest little girl. They even gave him extra candy for being so darn cute. I didn't get any extra candy. And I always have to share my Halloween candy with Katie because she is too old to go trick or treating. I enjoy the homemade popcorn balls the best.

We play hide and seek for a while after it gets dark. Katie is the seeker and Billie and I are hiding. I can hear Katie counting to fifty. Sneaking to the barn, I climb the ladder to the hay loft and hide. I hear Billie laughing when Katie finds him. He is usually easy to find. He always laughs the closer you get to him. *I don't think Katie will find me too easily in the barn. She knows I am frightened of the dark. I will fool her!*

"Billie, do you know where Missy is hiding? If you do and you tell me, I'll let you make the first phone call!"

I hear Billie whispering loudly to Katie as they come closer to the barn. All of a sudden I hear a loud crash as I watch my ladder to the hay loft fall to the bottom of the barn floor.

"Missy, if you are in the hay loft, you better tell us before we go into the house and leave you up there all night," Katie says laughing.

Billie chimes in, "Ha...Ha...Missy. We have you now!" Sandy starts barking at where the ladder used to stand. She doesn't think I should be up in the hay loft without her.

"Missy, if you like being up in the hay loft so much you can just sleep there in the dark by yourself!" Katie taunts me, as they slowly walk toward the house.

"Please come back. This isn't funny anymore. Put the ladder back so I can get down. You win, I'm up here hiding!"

"I suppose, but I ought to let you stay up there all night!"

"Yeah, we ought to let Missy stay up in the hay loft all night, right, Katie?" Billie giggles.

"Billie, help me put the ladder back, and let the little baby down. She did share some of her candy with us when we did the puzzle. Maybe if we let her down, she will give us each more candy later. Besides, we want to go in the house and make our prank phone calls, don't we?"

"I guess," Billie says hesitantly.

We go back into the house to make our calls. I am happy not to be sleeping in the dark barn all night. I'll gladly share the rest of my candy with Billie and Katie.

"Okay, Billie, I said you could make the first phone call. Do you remember what to say when someone answers?"

"When someone answers the phone I say, 'Hello, do you have Prince Albert in a can? If they say yes, I say, 'Well then you better go let him out. Is that okay, Katie?"

"That's it, Billie. You've got it!"

The first call Billie makes, no one is home. He almost starts crying. Tears well up in his eyes. Katie assures him he can continue calling people until someone answers. It takes about five calls before anyone knows what he is talking about. Billie is having so much fun Katie lets him call a few more people. One person actually swears at Billie and asks him if his parents know what he is doing. He hangs up on them fast. Katie says I can go next. Then we will each take turns.

I ask people if their refrigerator is running. If they answer yes, I tell them they better hurry up and fetch it before it gets away.

We continue our prank calls until about ten o'clock. The jokes are beginning to get old. The people we call aren't amused. We go back to working on our puzzle until midnight. Mama will love seeing the completed puzzle in the morning.

Chapter Eleven

It is hotter than the devil in the bedrooms upstairs. The air is stuffy, and I feel like someone is smothering me. I can't roll over in bed. The sheets are wet with sweat and sticking to my body.

There isn't any breeze coming in through the open window. Even the crickets are quiet. Once in a while you can hear a car drive past our house. I know eventually one of the cars will be Mama and Uncle Frank's.

I sleep for what seems like only minutes when I hear a car pull into our driveway. As the car door opens, I hear Mama and Uncle Frank giggling like teenagers.

"Oops, I must have tripped," Mama says, laughing and stumbling on the driveway.

Uncle Frank is trying to hold her up, but about every fifth step they both stumble. The next time she pulls Uncle Frank down with her. They both get back up after several tries and take a few more steps toward our garage door. *I hope none of the neighbors see them.*

As they reach the house, they fall and knock over the metal garbage cans. It makes such a racket the neighbor's black lab starts howling. With that, comes a chorus of all the other neighbor's dogs. Sandy usually doesn't chime in. Mama argued with Uncle Riley, but Sandy seems to be vicious when it comes to Uncle Frank fighting with Mama. Mama usually cuddles Sandy and holds on to her like a stuffed toy taunting Uncle Frank.

I can see a few lights going on in some of the neighbors' homes. I hope they don't call the police.

"Frank, you have to be quieter," Mama whispers quite loud. "The neighbors will hear us, shhh...."

Being quiet isn't Mama's best trait when she is drunk. Even when she whispers, you can hear her in the next room. Uncle Frank is never quiet. He doesn't even attempt to talk soft. He says real men don't whisper.

I swear I can smell alcohol on their breath from my upstairs bedroom window. They smell like they fell into a brewery.

There is a register in the floor where I can usually observe and hear what is going on in the kitchen. I lie down on the hot, sticky wood floor and watch through the register. It is almost as good as watching television if we had one to watch. The last time I saw television is when we went to Daddy's boss' house to watch the *Wizard of Oz* in color.

Mama and Uncle Frank get another bottle of beer from

the refrigerator and continue drinking. They just take a drink from their beer bottle and then puff on their cigarettes. Once in a while, I can see Uncle Frank blowing smoke rings to impress Mama. She has been blowing smoke rings for as long as I can remember. I even saw her smoke a long skinny cigar once.

After a few more beers, the laughing stops cold. Their voices grow steadily louder.

Sandy decides she isn't going to take Uncle Frank's yelling at Mama any longer. The fighting is getting far too serious. She starts snarling and growling at Uncle Frank. She wants him to know she means business. Uncle Frank kicks Sandy across the kitchen floor and makes her yelp.

"Frank, don't you ever touch my dog again. If she's hurt, you are going to pay the vet bill! Do you hear me?"

Frank is rattling on so fast I can't understand a word he says.

Mama holds onto her kitchen chair trying desperately to stand. She holds on to the table with one hand and smacks Uncle Frank with the other. "Get out of my house! Don't come back!"

Uncle Frank grabs Mama's arm so quick after she smacks him in the face, it causes her to lose her balance; falling to the kitchen floor with him still holding on to her arm.

"Frank, you're hurting me! Let go! Oww…let me go…."

"Dot, does it hurt?" Uncle Frank asks, jerking her arm harder. He shoves her face down onto the floor with her arm twisted behind her back. "One of these days I'm going to have to kill you! Tell me you're sorry!"

"I'll never tell you, oww...I'm oww... sorry... you bastard! Get out...oww...of my house now or I'm calling the police!"

Uncle Frank lets go of Mama's arm. She crawls to a chair to pull herself up from the floor. Then she stumbles over to the kitchen counter. She opens a drawer and pulls out a large rolling pin. "You bastard! You'll never touch me again!"

Uncle Frank staggers toward Mama and tries to grab her arm again. As he reaches for her arm, Mama swings the rolling pin with all her might. It lands smack in the middle of his ugly forehead. Uncle Frank falls backward. Blood oozes all over our clean kitchen floor. The small amount of hair on Uncle Frank's head is now crimson red. I think Mama killed Uncle Frank right there in our kitchen. She has blood all over her clothes and on her hands. She raises the rolling pin up ready to strike Uncle Frank again.

"Frank, get up I'm not through with you yet!" Mama yells.

Uncle Frank doesn't move. His eyes are red from blood trickling down his face. He just lies on our kitchen floor in his own blood, lifeless.

"Katie, get up. I think Mama's gone and killed Uncle Frank. He's lying dead on our kitchen floor. Get up, Katie!" I whisper, trying not to cry.

I try shaking her. "Hmm, what do you want, Missy?" A drowsy Katie asks as she turns over in bed.

"Katie, I'm serious. Please wake up. Mama's gone and killed Uncle Frank!"

"It's late, Missy. You just had a bad dream. Go back to sleep and let me get some rest."

"I'm serious, just come and look for yourself."

Katie climbs out of her bed and looks through the register on the floor.

"How do you know Mama killed him, Missy?"

"I saw her hit him in the head with her rolling pin."

"There sure is a lot of blood. I can't see if his eyes are open." Katie acknowledges.

Mama stares at Uncle Frank and says nothing. She doesn't move. Her usually tan face is pale.

"What do you think we should do? Do you think they'll put Mama in jail? Will we have to go to an orphanage? They'll probably split us up. Maybe we should wake Billie up and run away!" I cry.

"Quiet. Let me think for a minute." She takes a deep breath before continuing. "We better wake Billie up and help him pack his bags. Try to keep him quiet. We don't want Mama to know we saw anything yet. We'll wait until we know she isn't in shock. Do you hear me?"

"Yes, Katie. What about Uncle Frank?"

"Just pack your bags and don't tell Billie what you saw. We'll just tell him we are going to stay at Aunt May and Uncle Jimmy's for a week."

"Billie, wake up, we're going on a little vacation to Aunt

May and Uncle Jimmy's. You need to pack your bag. I'll help you. Gather up your army men and a couple of comic books. I'll start packing your clothes," Katie calmly tells him.

"I want to go to sleep. Wake me up in the morning," Billie says yawning. He could sleep through a tornado if one were to come through his bedroom window.

Katie shakes Billie again. "Billie, wake up! We have to pack tonight. I'll let you get dressed and then you better start packing your stuff."

We go back to the register to see if Mama has moved. *Maybe Mama wants us to help her bury Uncle Frank's body in our back yard.*

Mama is still sitting on the floor next to Uncle Frank. Tears are streaming down her face. There are streaks of Uncle Frank's blood on her face from wiping them. She was really mad at Uncle Frank, but I don't think she meant to kill him.

"Missy, I'm going to have to go down and help Mama. When you're finished packing your bags, help Billie pack his. Throw some clothes and makeup in a bag for me, too, would you?"

"Be careful, Katie. I'm not sure if Mama knows what she's doing. Try and get Sandy to come upstairs before Uncle Frank tries to kill her again—if he ever wakes up. He already tried kicking her to death!" I state.

"Don't worry. We're going to be all right. I will do everything possible to keep our family together!"

Katie sure can act mature when she has to. She makes me

feel safe. I know she won't let anyone separate our family. Maybe she is going to help Mama bury Uncle Frank's body. He is pretty heavy. I'm sure they will need my help. Maybe we can put him in my red wagon to carry him. We better bury him deep so Sandy doesn't dig him up.

Billie packs his toys while I pack the rest of his clothes. I make sure he has enough underwear and socks for a week. He wants to pack every comic book he owns, which must be close to a hundred. I finally convince him to pack ten.

"Missy, they lay flat and don't take much space. I don't need any socks. Please let me take them."

Billie never likes anyone touching his comic books. If he catches you looking at one of his comic books, he tears the cover off. He even tears the covers off his brand new comic books so you won't know they are new. I like to keep my books looking like they are brand new and never used even though most of them come from garage sales.

"Billie, what if we get some spending money and you purchase new comics; how will you bring them home?"

Finally, Billie gives in and packs what I ask. I think he is too tired to argue.

"If you want, you can go back to sleep until Katie and I are through packing our stuff, but you have to make sure Sandy stays in your room."

"That's a deal, Missy! Goodnight. I'm tired. We stayed up too late already," Billie says, as he wraps his arms tighter around Sandy's neck.

It isn't five minutes, and Billie and Sandy are sound asleep. *Good, then maybe Billie won't ever know we had to bury old Uncle Frank to save Mama from going to jail, and Sandy won't ever know where to dig up Uncle Frank's body. Maybe we can bury him in Mama's compost heap, that's where she puts a lot of her garbage to rot. Next summer old Uncle Frank might just be pushing up daisies.*

Billie looks peaceful sleeping in his bed. *I hope this won't be the last time I see him sleeping there.*

I go downstairs to help Katie and Mama bury old Uncle Frank. He must weigh at least two times what Mama weighs.

"Mama, are you all right? Mama, do you hear me?" A worried Katie asks.

"It's going to be okay, Mama. We'll help you. Tell us what you want us to do."

Finally, Mama turns to look at us. She starts crying hysterically. She turns toward Uncle Frank's body and just stares at it again. She is beginning to sober up now and must realize what she's done.

Mama stands staring at the bloody body on the kitchen floor. "I think I killed Frank!"

"Are you sure he's dead?" Katie asks.

Mama looks alert now. There is a glimmer of hope in her eyes.

She tries wiping some of the blood off of Uncle Frank's face. "Katie, we have to see if he has a pulse. Help me see if he is breathing. Oh God, let him be alive! What have I done?"

Mama checks Uncle Frank's pulse then listens to his chest.

I say a short prayer for all of us.

"Katie, call an ambulance, Frank's still alive. I can barely get a pulse. Tell them to hurry. Then help me wash up some of the blood. Oh God, what am I going to do? I don't want to lose you kids. I don't want to go to jail. Frank! Frank…wake up. You can't die on me. Please, wake up. Missy, go pack your bags. I'll see if Aunt May and Uncle Jimmy will come and get you kids until this mess is straightened out. Please hurry, we don't have much time."

"Mama, we already have our bags packed," Katie says. "We packed them before we came downstairs."

She looks confused but doesn't ask Katie any questions. There will be a lot of questions asked when the police and paramedics arrive. I pray to God that if old Uncle Frank is still alive, Mama doesn't go to jail and we don't go to any orphanage.

Mama and Katie clean up old Uncle Frank and all his blood on our kitchen floor. She puts a red checked oil cloth under his head to keep the blood from flowing on the freshly washed floor.

"You know girls; you need to stop listening to my conversations through the register upstairs. I'm glad you helped me with Frank, but one of these times you are going to get yourselves hurt."

"But Mama—"

"We can finish this conversation later. I need to call your Aunt May."

Mama barely gets through talking to Aunt May when we hear sirens. It doesn't sound like just a siren from an ambulance. It sounds like the whole police department!

All the neighbors' dogs are howling in unison. I'm sure the neighbors are awake by now. *It's too bad we just couldn't have buried old Uncle Frank quietly in our backyard. I saw them do it in the movies.*

You can hear the sirens for miles. When the police from the surrounding towns have a slow night, they listen to other police calls to get the latest gossip. They don't want to be the last to hear what happened the next day from Charlene, the waitress at Dixie's Donut Hole up the road.

It sounds like a parade on the Fourth of July with all the local police, fire, and ambulance sirens blaring. Maybe they figure Mama has gone and killed Uncle Frank for real this time. It sure will be a lot quieter around our house if she has.

We can hear Sandy howling from Billie's bedroom window. Lights are going on in bedrooms all around the neighborhood. *I will never be able to face any of our neighbors again.*

When Katie called for an ambulance, the dispatcher asked her a lot of questions she answered truthfully to the best of her knowledge. She told the dispatcher, "Mama hit Uncle Frank over the head with a rolling pin after he had pinned her face down on the kitchen floor. He had her arm twisted behind her back. They both had been drinking and were quarrelling before she hit him smack in the middle of his forehead!"

The dispatcher wanted to know if Uncle Frank was still

breathing. Katie told her Uncle Frank lost a lot of blood and is unconscious, but he still has a faint pulse. Then she tells them they had better arrive quickly.

When the ambulance arrives, the drivers put Uncle Frank on the stretcher and take him to Dixon Hospital. Mama can go there later to see how he is doing. First, she has to talk to the police.

Mama is friends with most of the police officers from the area. In fact, Uncle Riley is still the Chief of police. When Daddy died he assisted with all the necessary arrangements that come with an accidental death or at least that's what they called it. I heard Uncle Riley tell Mama they didn't have any proof someone ran him into the telephone pole, but it looked suspicious.

A very good looking police officer places his arm around Mama. "Damn, Dot, what did you go and try to kill Frank for? You could have just kicked him out and I would have taken care of you, darling!"

Another charming officer interrupts. "Uh hum—Dot, you should have known a rolling pin would do a lot of damage to that man of yours!"

"You sure got yourself in a pickle this time. You better hope Frank wakes up soon or I won't be able to help you out. Sit down and tell me what went on here tonight," Chief Riley tells Mama, as he points to a kitchen chair.

Chief Riley and some of his officers ask Mama questions for about an hour. Then they question Katie and me.

Aunt May and Uncle Jimmy arrive not long after the police and ambulance. They are escorted to the porch and are told to stay there until they are finished questioning all of us.

"Dot, do you need a ride to the hospital? I have to go there anyway and ask Frank some questions when he wakes up. In fact, this isn't the only case I need to discuss with Frank. You really should think about moving Frank out. I have a bad feeling about this man!" He says concerned, as he gives Mama a more than comforting hug.

"That would be nice, Riley. Thanks for wanting to protect us, but as you can see, I can handle myself. Jimmy and May are going to take the kids for the night. I just hope Frank lives. I don't know who will raise my kids. Jimmy and May have enough trouble raising their own!"

Uncle Riley ruffles my hair. "I'm always here for you and the kids, Dot. I need to know you are all safe. I'll finish up with the rest of the investigation, and then we'll leave. Do what you have to for your kids."

Everyone else is gone except a few police officers, Aunt May, and Uncle Jimmy. It is sure quiet in our kitchen now. Mama lets out a big sigh as she slumps into a kitchen chair. "What am I going to do, May? Frank has to be okay, I can't afford to miss work and I sure don't want to go to jail for killing him!"

"We can drop you off at the hospital and take the kids for the night if you want us to." Aunt May tells Mama. She hands her a freshly brewed, strong cup of coffee trying to sober her up. "You had best not drive yourself tonight, Hun!"

"Thanks, May, for all you're doing and coming out here in the middle of the night. Riley is going to take me to the hospital. He still has a few questions for Frank."

The tears start flowing down Mama's cheeks as she tells Aunt May and Uncle Jimmy what has taken place. Everyone can see the bruises on Mama's arms. She also has finger prints on her right wrist where Uncle Frank grabbed her and twisted her arm behind her back.

Aunt May straightens up the kitchen, not looking too happy about the whole situation. "Are your bags packed so we can go soon, kids?"

"We packed awhile ago, Aunt May," Katie says.

Aunt May turns her back to Katie and looks at Mama disgustingly. "Dot, you better freshen up a bit and put some clean clothes on before you go see Frank! You don't want anyone to see you looking like this do you?" Aunt May takes a puff of her old smelly cigarette. "Jimmy, make sure those kids are packed, and I'll get Dot moving!" She flicks her cigarette letting the ashes drop onto our clean kitchen table.

Someday Aunt May is going to burn our house down. She either has a cigarette in her hand or a cup of coffee. It doesn't matter what time of day it is. I guess her smoking on those cigarettes keeps her from eating everything in sight and getting as fat as an old cow. Uncle Jimmy always did say he won't stand for his woman to be fat and sassy like his Mama was.

Chapter Twelve

Riley takes Mama to the hospital in his car. We have to ride in Aunt May and Uncle Jimmy's old station wagon. Billie and Katie are asleep before we get a block away from home. I force myself to stay awake to see what future plans might await us.

Aunt May whispers. "Missy, you awake back there?"

"Yes, Aunt May, I'm awake," I answer yawning. "I can't help but worry about Mama."

"You better hope your Mama comes and gets you brats later today or you'll have to find someplace else to stay. I've got enough kids to feed and look after!"

I'm glad it's dark so Aunt May doesn't get the satisfaction of seeing tears flowing down my cheeks. Sometimes I think Aunt May just hates kids. When we stay at Aunt May's house, she makes us go to bed before eight on the weekends.

Aunt May and Uncle Jimmy stay in bed till noon. We aren't to disturb them. I sleep in Rita's bed. When we wake, she wants to know all the details of the night before. I exaggerate and tell her Mama killed Uncle Frank. I wasn't really lying because Uncle Frank might be dead by now. I'm sure we will all find out later when Mama calls.

Billie is lucky. He gets to sleep with Bobby. They have plenty of comic books to read to pass the time away. Some of them are even new.

Katie gets to sleep on the couch in the living room by herself. There is a black and white television set in that room. In the morning she can quietly turn on the television and watch cartoons. I imagine she might even make a telephone call to Charlie while everyone else is asleep. He will want to know all the details about Mama and old Uncle Frank.

We all have to wait to use the bathroom until Uncle Jimmy is done. He has a stash of books in the bathroom that could fill three shelves in our study. It takes him forever to come out of there. I'm thinking for sure I will wet my pants. I even contemplate going out behind one of the trees in their backyard; but their neighbors are closer than ours.

Aunt May and Uncle Jimmy sit at their red chrome kitchen table and drink two pots of coffee while they puff on their Camel cigarettes. We kids have cornflakes, milk, and toast for breakfast at noon. I'm not too hungry anyway. I am waiting for news from Mama. If the news is bad and old Uncle Frank is dead, I'm sure we will all go to an orphanage. We know kids who are orphans who go to our school. They already told us how much they hate living there.

It is around one in the afternoon when Mama finally calls Aunt May. For us kids it seems like a lifetime. We can only hear one side of the conversation, but we still figure out old Uncle Frank is alive and as well as can be expected with him getting hit over the head with a rolling pin. He is coming home soon. Chief Riley is at the hospital still taking statements from Mama and Uncle Frank.

When the hospital releases Uncle Frank, Uncle Riley takes them home. I sure like Uncle Riley. It is too bad he isn't still our uncle. Aunt May will take us home later, after Mama has time to settle Uncle Frank in.

Katie, Billie, and I look at each other relieved. We are sure glad we don't have to spend another night at Aunt May's. *I am glad Uncle Frank isn't dead so Mama doesn't have to go to jail and we don't have to go to an orphanage, but I sure wish he was going home to any house but ours.*

Katie is in a hurry to get home. She has a date with Charlie tomorrow. They are going to go to the outdoor movie theater with some of their friends to watch a new Dracula flick. She knows if she can't go, Charlie will take someone else. Now she will have enough time to set her hair with her big bristly rollers and paint her nails.

Aunt May makes her special Hungarian Chicken Paprikash, homemade Hungarian noodles and fresh baked bread before she takes us home. It takes her almost three hours to cook her special meal. She says it's because she makes it with love. She looks so happy cutting every noodle out while she sings country western songs along with the radio. There is a beautiful breeze coming from the kitchen window which makes the aroma of the bread baking heavenly. All the different smells of the food is making my mouth water.

Aunt May's Hungarian Chicken Paprikash is one recipe Mama hasn't mastered. Aunt May says the secret to her recipe is using the best sweet Hungarian paprika she can afford. The meal usually is served at Easter or Christmas. *I guess Mama not killing old Uncle Frank and Aunt May not having to worry about taking care of us kids is a special occasion.*

Uncle Frank is in bed when we get home. He says he feels like a truck has run him over. His head is black and blue and as large as one of the pumpkins on doorsteps at Halloween; all smashed in.

Mama is sure happy to be home. I think she thought she was never going to see our house again.

She is all dressed up in some new clothes Uncle Frank purchased for her the week before. She looks like a million bucks!

"May, you shouldn't have gone to all the trouble of fixing your special Hungarian Chicken Paprikash. You have done enough just taking care of the kids for a spell. How can I ever thank you?"

"Dot, the only thing I want is for you to sit yourself down at that table and eat with us. I'm just glad you're home to take care of your kids. Lord, I have enough trouble taking care of my own!" Aunt May says matter of fact.

Mama takes in all the aromas of Aunt May's special dinner. She helps Aunt May set the table so we can have a feast fit for a queen. Uncle Frank still doesn't have an appetite. Uncle Jimmy says it is okay with him. He will just eat Uncle Frank's share of the food. I don't know how Uncle Jimmy stays so skinny.

We eat until our stomachs are about to explode. Our meal never tasted better. We have a lot to celebrate.

The next day Mama and Uncle Frank are back to sitting in the red velvet, overstuffed chair in the living room kissing and making out like there is no tomorrow. Uncle Frank's head looks like a rotting pumpkin. I don't know how anyone can look at him let alone kiss him.

Katie gets ready to go on her date with Charlie and his friends. She is extra nice to me and Billie since Mama hit old Uncle Frank in the head with the rolling pin. I think she is feeling protective of us.

"Mama, can Missy and Billie go to the movies with Charlie and me? We are going to see *Kiss of the Vampire*, over in Dixon. We promise we won't do anything stupid!" Katie pleads.

"Are you sure you're not going to drop those kids off somewhere, Katie? I don't want to have to go looking for any kids tonight. I told Frank we are just going to have a nice quiet evening at home."

"Mama, with all of us kids gone it will be nice and quiet

for you," Katie suggests.

"I suppose. I don't want any speeding and I don't have much money to give you for treats at the concession stand. You'll have to make yourselves some popcorn to take with."

"Thanks for letting them go. I promise we'll be good and don't worry about us. You just relax and enjoy yourself!"

Uncle Frank calls us over to the chair he is sitting in. He whispers. "If you kids cause any trouble tonight, your Mama won't have to buy fish bait the next time she goes fishing, you'll be the bait. I don't know why you couldn't just stay at May and Jimmy's. Your Mama and I get along just fine when you kids aren't around. Too bad for you I didn't die!"

Katie looks at Billie and me. "We won't cause any trouble, Uncle Frank!"

I am glad I don't have to sit around and watch Mama and Uncle Frank kiss all night, but I'm not sure about watching a vampire film. I think the movie and old Uncle Frank will give me nightmares. I will have to sleep with the covers over my head for a week.

Chapter Thirteen

Katie and I pop popcorn to take to the outdoor theater. We fill four brown paper bags full and top each one with lots of butter and salt. Mama gives us each some money for a soda pop, but I'm not too sure I want anything to drink.

"Missy, Billie, you better bring a pillow and blanket in case you want to sit outside to watch the film," Katie suggests.

"That's a great idea. I sure won't want to stay in the back seat of the hot old stuffy car and watch you and Charlie kissing all night!"

"Me, neither!" pipes up Billie. "I get enough of watching that mushy stuff from Mama and Uncle Frank."

"You two just cut it out right now or I'm not taking you with. Do you hear me? Maybe I should just leave you home with old Uncle Frank!" Katie says aggravated.

"Okay, Okay, we won't bother you. But what if I have to go to the bathroom?" I ask.

"You'll either go by yourself or you'll have to wait for

intermission."

Katie and Charlie can have the whole car to themselves. Billie and I will just sit out on the gravel on blankets and not bother them. We are just lucky they are allowing us to go to the movies.

It is taking longer than usual to get through the gates at the outdoor theater. The car in front of us is being searched by attendants to see if there are any extra kids hiding under blankets or in the trunk. How the theater knows kids are hiding is beyond me. I counted six kids in the car and three more popped out of the trunk. They make them all pay and then they let them go through the gate. *They sure must not be scared of the dark to be in the trunk.*

We watch previews of upcoming movies in the car with Katie and Charlie. We all agree that when Alfred Hitchcock's *The Birds* comes to the theater we will go see it together. Being attacked by birds won't frighten me as much as vampires; my Grandma Irene has pet parakeets.

At dusk, everyone starts honking their horns and flashing their headlights for the movie to begin. I enjoy this part of the theater. It makes my heart pound with anticipation.

"You guys have to take your blankets and popcorn outside now. The movie is about to start." Katie says smiling.

"Okay, Okay, we're going. We'll get a better breeze out there anyway. It's hot in the back seat!" I say, as I slide out between the seats.

• • •

There are quite a few kids sitting on blankets in front of vehicles, in back of trucks, and on top of cars. This makes me feel a lot safer. There will be a lot of victims for the vampires to choose from. Mama told us kids when she was younger; a vampire attacked a girl around here somewhere and drank all her blood. I'm not going to let that happen to me or Billie.

When the previews start, I inch closer to Billie. With only having two blankets I might need one to cover my head when the movie starts. Billie doesn't mind. He has already eaten half of his bag of popcorn and wants to know if he can share some of mine later.

The movie is set in Bavaria in 1910. A couple on their honeymoon are driving on an old dirt road in the middle of nowhere, when they discover that they are lost, running out of gas, and nothing is around them but a dark scary wooded area.

They end up at a hotel with one other guest; an alcoholic professor. They get a letter requesting they join Dr. Ravna for dinner at his castle in the mountains. The inn keepers urged them to do so.

For the first half of the movie, I make it without anything to drink or going to the bathroom. I don't even cover my head too much. Just as the movie begins getting scary, I get thirsty and decide I can't wait any longer to go pee. *I know Katie won't take me. In fact, I don't think Charlie and Katie even remember we are along.*

"Billie, will you go with me to the restroom? We can get us

a soda at the concession stand. Please? I don't think I can wait for intermission!"

"I guess, but it's at the good part now."

"We can watch the screen all the way to the concession stand and you can still see the movie from inside, through the big picture window. If you get both our drinks, it won't take us as long."

We walk quietly in the dark to the concession stand, keeping our eyes on the screen all the way there. When we get in front of one of the big light poles close to the women's restroom, a bat flies over us.

"Billie, run, it's a vampire!" I scream so loud the girl in the car next to me screams, too. This let out a chain reaction of screams which frightens me even more as I watch a vampire on the screen get attacked.

Horns start blaring all around us and people begin hollering for us to be quiet.

Billie makes it to the front of the women's restroom before me.

"Missy, are you all right? Did the bat bite you?" he asks, out of breath and frightened. "You're not going to turn into one of those vampires, are you?"

"No. I think the screams scared him off, and I'm definitely not turning into any blood thirsty vampire!"

"I'll wait right here for you, Missy. Make it quick. I'm scared the vampire will come back and attack us!"

I don't know how I made it to the bathroom. When I saw

the bat flying over my head, it almost scared me to death. Maybe the bat can find someone else to drink blood from and leave Billie and me alone.

Billie and I go inside the concession stand together to get our soda pop. When the girl behind the counter is making our drinks, someone comes up from behind us and taps me on the shoulder.

I let out a scream that can be heard all over the theater. The girl behind the counter jumps about ten feet and drops our soda pops on the floor.

Katie's hands are firmly planted on her hips like Mama's. "Are you two all right? I heard you scream clean from Charlie's car. What on earth happened? You're making me miss the movie!"

Billie rattles on as fast as he can get the words out of his mouth. "We saw a bat. It was going to turn into a vampire...and drink our blood...right there on the spot!"

An older lady next to us started roaring with laughter. I thought for sure she was going to drop dead; she is bent over and holding her side.

"Get your drinks. I'll walk you both back to the car. And don't leave my sight again. You already embarrassed me enough for one night!" Katie says sternly.

Katie holds her head high. She doesn't even pay attention to all the people staring at us as we walk out the door. *Katie is just mad because we interrupted her and Charlie kissing. I don't know if she even knows what the movie is really about.*

Chapter Fourteen

We are going to go to Grandma Irene's fifty-eighth birthday party. Step-Grandpa Roy McCaffey will probably get drunk as usual. He is Irish with red hair and a fiery temper to match. I never like going to Grandma Irene's house much when he is there. It is like watching a storm brewing for hours, and when it finally hits, it is full-force.

They live on a farm in Oregon, Illinois about twenty minutes from our house. They have about 500 acres they farm. Grandma Irene works real hard. I don't think she ever gets any rest. She is thin and looks like she is a lot older than she really is.

Roy is a few years younger than Grandma Irene. No one ever mentions his exact age to us, so we really don't know how much younger he is. His hair is starting to turn strawberry-blond. He won't get gray like Grandma. He is tan and has a lot of freckles on his arms. Sometimes I can't tell if he has a tan or is just one big freckle. He has a lot of muscles from putting up hay and straw, and working on the farm when he isn't drinking or beating Grandma. I don't know why she stays with him. She has more yellow and green bruises on her arms and legs than most of Mama's apples she cans.

Their farm house has the old asphalt shingles and no bathroom. If we want water, we have to go outside to the well and pump it. There is a wood burning stove in the kitchen. It gives everything Grandma makes a marvelous smoky flavor that makes me drool.

They heat their entire house with wood to save on money. There isn't any carpet on the floors. All the rugs are made by Grandma Irene. She has the most beautiful rag rugs and braided rugs on her floors I ever did see anywhere. There are more colors in her quilts than in my colored pencil box.

All the quilts on her beds are made by her. She doesn't waste anything. She will go to garage sales and purchase clothes for hardly anything to make her quilts and rugs. Some of the church women donated items they couldn't salvage for Grandma to use for her quilts. She even has some material and some old clothes saved from her Mama. She always puts a small square of the material in each of her quilts she makes. This is her signature and reminds her of her childhood.

Grandma's curtains are made out of old tablecloths and dishtowels. Someone's trash is always Grandma's treasure. Roy never gives Grandma much money. Being a farmer, he says he is too poor. He sure can find money for beer and cigarettes though.

• • •

They have two old geese, Herbert and Mary. Every time I go to Grandma's house those two old geese follow me around and terrorize me. They run after me honking the whole way. One time, Herbert bit my leg when he caught me. That really hurt!

We always have fresh brown eggs from Grandma Irene's hen house. Her favorite chickens, Rhode Island Reds, produce the best tasting eggs, and the yolks are always a darker yellow than the stores. Grandma will go out to the hen house with her Mama's wire basket early in the morning to fetch eggs. Those Rhode Island Reds lay between 14 and 18 eggs every day. They will just be waiting at the old hen house for Grandma in the morning. When she enters the pen, they all swarm around her feet waiting for her attention. I almost feel sorry for those hens losing their eggs until I remember how good they taste.

I like my eggs over easy so I can dip my toast in the runny yolks. I sprinkle lots of pepper on my eggs, which always makes me sneeze. I don't care. This is the way those eggs taste best. Katie says she wants to throw up watching me eat them.

We are going to have fried chicken at Grandma Irene's for dinner. Grandma Irene, Aunt May, and Mama are all going to cook up the chickens.

First, we have to catch the old hens that are going to be our dinner today. Those chickens sure must know they are going to be butchered because they make a lot of racket and keep running around in circles to avoid us. We are going to fry those three old hens up in cast-iron skillets on Grandma's wood stove.

I don't much care for killing and cleaning those chickens. Grandma Irene has an old stump in the back yard they use for chopping the chickens' heads off.

Herbert and Mary come to watch some of their old barnyard friends get their heads chopped off. They are following Grandma around honking and carrying on.

Grandma chases her geese around the stump with a broom. "Herbert and Mary, you go on now and get out of here or we'll have you for dinner tonight instead!"

"Jimmy, you best stretch the chicken's head over that stump so Roy can get a clean shot at chopping its head off the first time."

Roy sharpens his ax the night before he chops the chicken's neck off. I never did see such a sight before. The chicken just keeps hopping around all over the barnyard without her head, blood squirting everywhere. We kids have to help with the plucking of the feathers; those chickens sure stink!

Uncle Frank just watches. He has never seen a chicken killed before. He asks if he can chop off the next chicken's head, but Roy tells him he never lets anyone else touch his chickens. Uncle Frank looks disappointed.

Those chickens are going to taste good later on when they coat them with flour, salt, pepper, and their secret ingredients.

After they are coated, they fry them all in fresh lard.

Mama made her potato salad the night before to bring. Aunt May brought baked beans. Uncle Frank is going to boil the corn again. *I'm sure that isn't going to make him happy.*

Mama, Aunt May, and Grandma Irene are going to bake corn bread in her wood stove. They are also going to bake Grandma's favorite chocolate cake made with coffee, cocoa, and mayonnaise. Grandma Irene's coffee is so strong she probably could flavor ten cakes with it. After the cake cools, Grandma will make whipping cream for the topping; using fresh cream from her cows.

"Mama, can I stay in and help bake the bread and make Grandma's birthday cake?" Katie asks.

"Katie, I would love for you to help bake! It's about time you learned to do a little cooking to help your Mama out," Grandma tells Katie before Mama can even answer.

Rita, Bobby, Billie, and I decide to go outside and play. We don't want any part of cooking.

Mama…Grandma, can we take a walk through your woods?" I ask.

"Scoot, off with ya," Grandma Irene says.

"If it's okay with your Grandma, then it's okay with me. You had better not get into any trouble!" Mama tells all of us kids.

"Now don't you kids be gone too long. We'll be eating in a couple of hours!" Aunt May instructs us sternly.

"Mama, do you think we can have a basket to put stuff in

if we find anything? Maybe we can find some flowers to give Grandma for her birthday!"

"That's a good idea, Missy! There are usually some wild flowers down by the creek this time of year."

Billie pipes up, "I want to go down by the creek!"

"I want to go to the creek, too!" Bobby chimes in.

Mama whispers. "Boys, I never said anything about going to the creek. I said there might be some flowers for your Grandma Irene down by the creek."

"You boys had better not go in that creek!" Aunt May says, not hearing any of the conversation.

"May, they're not going in the creek. Don't worry," Mama laughs. "For goodness sake, off with you before this conversation turns into you boys having already fallen into that creek!"

"You know, girls, Caroline's coming over later for supper."

"Mother, she always causes trouble when men are around. Not on your birthday," Aunt May cries out frustrated.

"You girls know she's Roy's daughter and I can't say no. Now, I don't want to hear anymore whining from either of you!"

"Mother, she never brings any food, she never helps you, and she drinks as much as Roy!" Aunt May comments worried.

"Hush with you, let's just try to forget about Caroline until later on. Don't you girls' go talking about Roy like that anymore. He really is a good man!"

"Good for nothing!" Mama says under her breath.

"What did you say, Dot?"

"Nothing Mother, nothing at all."

Aunt May coughed. "Yeah, she said nothing at all."

"You girls' hush or I'm going to send you to the woods with those kids of yours."

"Katie, what are we going to do about your Mama?" Grandma Irene asks her.

Katie winks. "Let's ground her for two weeks so she can't see her boyfriend, Grandma."

"I'd like to see you try and ground me, either of you!" Mama tells them both.

"I guess I couldn't do anything with you girls when you lived at home. You just climbed out the window and down our tree. It wouldn't do me any good to try now!" Grandma tells Aunt May and Mama.

"Mother, don't say things like that in front of Katie; you might give her ideas!"

"Off with you kids. I thought you were going to the woods!" Mama tells all of us.

"We were, but we rather enjoyed the thought of Grandma grounding you and Aunt May at your age. We wanted to see if she could really still do it," I say laughing.

"Okay…outside…go play…you've heard enough stories for one day," Aunt May says to us kids. We know we had better get going before she changes her mind.

"Can we play cowboys and Indians, Missy?"

"Billie, no one wants to play cowboys and Indians."

"How about we make a fort out of branches?" Bobby asks.

"Bobby, I don't want to play in no dirty fort!" Rita says disgusted.

"How about we follow the path to the creek and when we get there, we can skip rocks," I suggest.

"That's a deal!" Bobby says. "But can we make it a contest to see who can skip their rock the farthest?"

Rita and I just give each other that look like, why does everything have to be a competition? The boys know we usually lose.

"We suppose," we said.

"Do you think there are any bear in these woods?"

"Billie, stop asking dumb questions. No, there aren't any bear in the woods around here," I tell him.

"Don't forget, we are supposed to be looking for flowers for Grandma's birthday on our walk to the creek," Rita says happily.

Rita spends more time with Grandma Irene than the rest of us. She likes to help Grandma cook and collect eggs in the mornings. Grandma is teaching her to garden. She especially wants to learn how to can pickles and beets like Grandma. They are her favorite. I don't spend the night much. I don't much care to use the chamber pot or the outhouse in the dark.

The boys don't care much to spend the night, either; Roy makes them work too hard.

Katie really doesn't like staying at the farm either. There aren't any boys around her age.

When we reach the creek, we find a tree that has been struck by lightning and has fallen over the creek. The water under the log isn't too deep, so we aren't worried about falling off and drowning. We just want to see how well we can balance on the old log.

Bobby goes first. He thinks he is going to be our hero and rescue us if we fall off. I will show him. No boy is going to out do me! I sure can't wear shoes and keep my balance. I take my shoes off and go barefoot. Splinters or not, I need to be able to use my toes to hang on.

"Come on, Missy, let's see you do it!" Bobby and Billie taunt me. Rita doesn't say a word against the boys.

As I step on the log, it begins rolling. My heart races. I think for sure I am going to fall. The log is narrow at the beginning and wider toward the middle. After the first couple of steps, I think I make it. Then Billie takes one end of the log and Bobby grabs a hold of the other end and starts rolling it back and forth to make me fall.

"You guys, stop it. This isn't funny. I'm going to get even with you when I get off this log!"

I sit down on the log and don't move. No one is going to make me fall in the creek and get into trouble, especially with Roy. I don't like him at all. He is mean to me and even worse to Grandma Irene. I don't want any bruises like he gives her!

"I'm not moving until you boys stop rolling this log, even if it takes all day!"

"Missy, you're no fun. Okay, we'll let you off," Bobby says amused.

"Aww…do we have to, Bobby?" Billie asks.

"I think we better."

I don't have any problem crossing the log when it isn't rolling. I walk across the whole log without even scooting. Rita just scoots across. She isn't even trying to walk across. She knows she has no balance.

Billie has no problem crossing the log either. He even wore shoes.

After we cross the log, we all look for the best flat rocks we can find to skip across the creek. *This is going to be fun. I have been practicing skipping rocks secretly at the river. If these boys want a competition, I am going to give them one. I'm not going to lose this time!*

"Now, don't go too close to the creek and get muddy, boys," I say.

The boys think they know everything about skipping rocks, but I'll show them.

"Okay, everyone line up right here along this bank," Bobby tells us.

"When I say three, everyone skip their rocks at the same time," he directs.

"One…Two…Three…"

Billie smiles at me. "Missy won! Missy won!"

"Something's not right here. Missy, did you step closer?"

"No, I didn't step closer. I won fair and square!"

"Let's try it again. Rita, will you watch to see who wins? Bobby asks his sister.

"I guess. Billie and I don't have a chance anyway."

"I'll go again, but I won. You're being a poor sport, Bobby!" I tell him, aggravated at him for not believing I didn't cheat.

"Are you ready?" Rita asks us.

"We're ready."

"One...two...three...go."

"Missy won! Missy won! I told you she won," Billie smiles at me.

"All right, I guess you won, but I don't know how you did it. I must have had a bad rock."

"Ah, forget it; let's go find Grandma Irene some flowers, Bobby," Rita says.

"Let's follow the creek for a ways. Mama said there should be some flowers around here somewhere."

"I saw some tall flowers by the back of the barn, Missy," Bobby says.

"I don't think Roy wants us to pick his sunflowers he planted, Bobby. Besides, they won't have blooms until we start back to school."

"What about those flowers," Billie says, pointing to something white up by the path.

"That's Queen Anne's Lace. Mama doesn't like it much, but it's sure pretty like the doilies Grandma Irene makes. It does have the word queen in its name," I say.

"They're white as snow and look like snow flakes." Rita remarks, as she picks the flowers and puts them into Grandma Irene's basket.

"Missy, I think they look more like the doilies Grandma crochets than snowflakes," Billie says. He taps me on the shoulder. "I thought you told me there are no bear in these woods!"

"There aren't any bears in this part of Illinois. Now quit being a baby and keep walking. It must be about dinner time by now. We still have to find more flowers for Grandma's bouquet."

"But, Missy…"

"What now?"

"What does a bear look like?"

"It doesn't matter, just keep on walking."

"Are bears black with a lot of short thick black fur?"

"Yeah, but there aren't any bears around here."

"Missy…Bobby…Rita…run. There's a bear!" Billie screams, pointing to a big black bear as he runs toward Grandma's house.

"Bobby, climb the nearest tree!" I shout, as I keep running.

Rita runs down the path toward Grandma's house tightly hanging on to her basket. "Help, there's a bear! Help, someone!"

"Rita, stop! We can't leave Bobby. Find some big rocks. We'll throw them at the bear. We have to save your brother!"

I shout, while trying to catch my breath.

The bear is at the bottom of the tree Bobby is in. It won't be long before the bear takes a hold of him and maybe even kills him. *We need to find a way to save Bobby fast!*

"We need to distract the bear. Billie. Make as much racket as you can. Scream, whistle, do anything!"

We see Bobby climbing down the tree.

"No, Bobby. Stop! Wait till we scare the bear away!" I scream at the top of my lungs.

Bobby laughs hysterically. "It's not a bear, Missy! It's Grandma Irene's dog, Bear."

Rita runs and gives Bear a great big hug, ruffling his fur. "Oh Bear, you scared us. Where were you, you naughty dog?"

Bear is Grandma Irene's old black Chow Chow. They usually put him in the barn when they have company. He is protective of his property. He likes Rita best; he has been around her more. When Bear gives you kisses, he kisses you with his big black tongue.

"I wonder if Grandma knows where you are, Bear? You scared us half-to-death. Come on; let's take you back to the barn," Rita tells Bear. She bends down to retrieve the flowers that had fallen out of her basket.

Bobby points to something yellow in the distance. "Hey, Rita, there's some flowers over by that old John Deere tractor."

"Bobby, thanks, those are black-eyed Susans. Grandma's going to like them!"

"Why do they call these flowers black-eyed Susans, Rita? They look like a daisy to me with dark-brown centers," Bobby states.

"I don't know, but they'll make a nice bouquet with the Queen Anne's lace."

We put Bear back in the barn; I don't think he is too happy. He just laid down on his straw bed and batted his eyes at us.

Rita hands Grandma her basket. "We picked flowers for your birthday!"

We see tears welling up in Grandma's eyes as she takes the basket of flowers. She lovingly looks at the Queen Anne's lace.

"You girls have the best kids in the world. They are so thoughtful and considerate. You ought to be thankful they're not out causing trouble!"

"You kids come over here and give me a hug, and then we'll go find these flowers a vase fit for a queen."

Bobby and Billie just look at each other. We know they will be getting a big kiss on their cheeks from Grandma. Rita and I don't mind much, but those boys' faces sure do turn red.

Grandma grins from ear to ear. "Now, off with you kids to the pump. We are going to eat soon."

"Your house sure does smell good, Grandma," Rita says.

Katie boasts. "I made Grandma's cake by myself!"

Grandma winks at Mama. "You sure did. It looks and smells wonderful. No one will ever want my cake again after they eat yours!"

Pleasing Grandma Irene isn't something that happens often. We all know Katie can be proud of herself today. You can tell Mama is proud of her daughter today, too.

"Boys, go out and tell the men folk to wash up. It's time to eat, and we don't want this dinner to get cold. You girls can pour us all some fresh milk," Grandma directs.

We do as we are told. We can't wait to eat. The food smells so good and we are hungry after all our exercise running from Bear.

"Grandma, Caroline's here," Bobby informs her. "Roy said to tell you to set another place for dinner."

"Not Caroline, not at dinner time! That girl sure does have bad timing. Just as I said, she never does a thing but impose. You better set another place at the table, Rita. Don't forget to pour her some milk. Maybe it will help her from getting drunk later on!" Aunt May says fuming.

"May, let's have a pleasant meal. If you can't be pleasant to Caroline, then do it for my birthday!" Grandma pleads.

"Rita, set Caroline's place next to Roy's, will ya, honey?" Grandma walks up to Caroline and gives her a kiss on the cheek. "I'm glad you could make it, dear."

"Isn't my girl pretty today, Ma?" Roy asks.

"Sure is, almost as pretty as the bouquet of flowers on the table the kids picked for me today."

"Oh, you guys, stop now; if only it were true, Papa,"

Caroline says blushing.

Uncle Frank and Uncle Jimmy must think she is pretty, too. Uncle Frank pulls out the chair for Caroline to sit in, and Uncle Jimmy asks her if there is anything else she needs. I haven't heard either of them ask to do anything for Mama or Aunt May today. Mama and Aunt May are already looking a might bit angry at those two men.

This is the best meal I have eaten in a long time, except our family's fish fry. Katie's cake is really good. It possibly might be better than Grandma Irene's, but I'm sure not going to tell either of them that.

Uncle Frank, Uncle Jimmy, and Roy are all more attentive to Caroline than to Grandma on her special day. Roy just keeps on having Grandma get this for him and that for him. I don't think she sits for a minute at our meal. He sure doesn't do anything for her. He just keeps talking to Caroline like no one else is around. You can almost feel the air around us getting colder and colder, even though it must be 85 degrees outside and even hotter inside from all the cooking.

"Mama, can I be excused? I have to go to the outhouse."

"While you're outside, Missy, can you pump some water for the dishes?"

"Sure. Do you want two buckets?"

"Maybe you better pump three. We sure do have a lot of dishes to wash with all this cooking today."

"Can I go with Missy, Grandma?" Rita asks.

"I guess; I think Missy might need some extra help with the buckets. But you girls make sure you don't dilly dally, ya hear me?"

"Yes, Grandma."

"I'll start getting the buckets of water, Missy, while you go use the outhouse."

"Okay, but don't go back in the house without me."

The old gray outhouse smells something awful. Grandma teases us and tells us she is so poor she just might leave some old corn cobs in the outhouse for us to use as toilet paper. The thought just makes me quiver. She told us, "When I was a young girl, we even used the *Sears Catalog* for toilet paper. You kids sure have it easy nowadays!"

At night, we take a flashlight out to that outhouse, unless Grandma is out of batteries; then we use candles. It gets mighty cold in the winter. Sometimes I think my butt is going to freeze right to the toilet lid. It sure does make you hurry, though.

I go into the old outhouse determined not to smell a thing. I only want to remember the smells of all the food in Grandma's house.

I sit down on the hot, sticky, toilet seat. There is a burning sensation in the right cheek of my tender butt. It feels like someone has just given me a penicillin shot. I hear an awful buzzing by my head. I don't even pull my pants up. I run out of that old outhouse screaming.

"Help! Bees are attacking me! Help, someone! Ouch!

Ouch! Rita, throw a bucket of water at those bees, and then run as fast as you can to the house!"

Everyone comes running out of the house. I swat at the bees the whole time I try pulling my pants up. Those darn bees sting me two more times. Everyone else laughs so hard they double over. Maybe if I'm lucky, one of them will use the outhouse, too!

"It's not funny. Mama, make them stop laughing. These bee stings hurt!"

Mama laughs. "Okay, off with you all. Leave Missy alone. You've had your laugh. Now go on about your business!"

Grandma glares at Roy. "Maybe you men better go see what you can do with those bees in the outhouse. Make yourselves useful!"

"Mama, it hurts something awful. I don't think I'll be able to sit for a week. They stung my arm twice!" I whine.

"I'll get some ice and an old towel. You go in and lay on my bed for a while on your stomach. I'll have your Mama bring you in the ice. I told Roy to check the outhouse before company arrived. I'm sorry, honey, there were bees in there. We'll do the dishes and you can just rest," Grandma tells me concerned.

"Thank you, Grandma." I'm almost glad I got stung in my butt by those darn bees. Now, I don't have to dry dishes for an hour in the hot kitchen.

I must have fallen asleep for a couple of hours. When I wake up, I hear voices coming from outside and my pants are wet. Thank goodness it isn't from me wetting Grandma's bed. Roy would sure whip me with a belt no matter what Mama says. *Thank goodness it's just the ice. It melted on my clothes while I slept.*

Uncle Jimmy, Uncle Frank, and Roy are using a bow and shooting arrows into bales of hay. They are supposed to aim for the bull's-eye which has been painted on one of the bales in the middle.

Roy and Uncle Jimmy have a bottle of beer in one hand while they try directing Uncle Frank on how to shoot the arrow. His arrow just falls four feet in front of him. It veers off to the left, and then it veers off to the right. It never once comes close to the target.

Caroline takes a big swig of her beer. "Honey, let me help you with your bow!"

She goes over to him and slowly shows him how to hold his bow getting as close behind him as she can; she positions his arms on the bow.

"Stand with your body at a right angle to the target, which is the bale of hay with the bull's-eye painted on it, not Dot. Put your left shoulder toward your target," Caroline tells Uncle Frank, as she turns his shoulder.

"Now, stand with your target slightly to the front of the line running from your left shoulder. Hold the bow in your left hand. Extend your left arm toward the target with your head in position looking at the target." She continues to direct

Uncle Frank as she puts her hands on both sides of his face, daring Mama to say something.

Caroline smiles. "Oh, Frank, you look even cuter the closer I get to you, sweetheart!"

I can see Mama's face getting redder and redder. She just might take the bow and arrow and use it on old Uncle Frank for letting Caroline getting so close.

"Now, Frank, honey, just place the arrow on the left-hand side of your bow with the odd-colored feather facing left; notch the arrow on the string, and then pull the string using your first three fingers of your right hand with the arrow between your first and second fingers. Keep your left arm, which is holding the bow, slightly bent. Keep your bow straight up and down. Now, pull the string to your face, aim your arrow at the middle of the target and let that baby go!"

Uncle Frank's arrow comes closer to the bull's-eye this time. But he still needs a lot of practice. Caroline goes hunting with Roy and belongs to an archery club, so she can hit the bull's-eye every time.

Mama guzzles her beer. You can feel the tension, and the air is getting thicker by the minute. "I think Frank's had enough lessons for one day, Caroline, don't you?"

"Frank, I think it's my turn now!" Mama tells him. She extends her arm out for the bow.

"Okay...okay. My arm is getting sore anyway!"

Uncle Frank goes over and stands by Caroline. He isn't too smart. Mama can shoot the arrow just as well as Caroline.

From the look on Mama's face, old Uncle Frank might be her next target. This time, he just might not make it out alive!

"Frank, do you want me to teach you how to shoot, or maybe you just want me to see how fast you can run before I make you my target?"

"Dot, let's be nice now. After all, this is my birthday party. I don't want any trouble. Maybe we should just put the bow and arrows away!" Grandma Irene says.

I think Grandma is worried Mama might actually shoot Uncle Frank or Caroline, or maybe even both.

"Yeah, Dot, we don't want anyone getting hurt!" Uncle Frank taunts Mama.

Caroline begins teasing Uncle Frank. "You're not going to let little old Dot scare you, are you, Hun?"

"Why don't you men go play horseshoes for a while? Caroline and I will go get you all another beer to cool off. Won't we Caroline?" Grandma says aggravated.

"How about bringing me my bottle of brandy, Caroline? It's in the cupboard with the coffee."

"Now, Roy, you don't want to start drinking brandy this early, do you?" Grandma asks.

"You heard me, Caroline. You don't have to listen to Irene. She's not your Mama. Bring me out my bottle of brandy, honey!"

I can see tears welling up in Grandma's eyes. She pretends something flew in them, but there is no wind, and I don't see any bugs flying around her.

Uncle Frank is pretty good at horseshoes. He wins every game. He does whine about how sore his arm is. No one else complains. Being an engineer draftsman and just sitting at his drafting table all day must make him soft. The only exercise he gets is his fingers pushing a pencil around all day.

Caroline proceeds to massage Uncle Frank's shoulders. "Poor, Frank. Where does it hurt, honey?"

"Oh…right there, where your hands are on my shoulders. Oh…that feels real good!"

"Papa, can you be a dear and hand me my beer?"

"For you, honey, I'll do anything!"

"I'll take one of those massages when you're done with Frank, Caroline!" Uncle Jimmy tells her.

"Oh, no you won't, you old fool!" Aunt May shouts at Uncle Jimmy. "You best just sit your ass right back down in your chair and mind your own business!"

Us kids decide the tension is getting to be too much sitting in Grandma Irene's green wicker chairs with all the grown ups drinking. We walk over to the picnic table and play cards. There is too much arguing going on over there and it isn't even dark yet.

We hear the arguing from the picnic table, but at least we aren't in the way of any beer bottles that might be thrown. Now and then we hear, "Bring me another beer," from one of the men. Then they all holler, "Me, too!" It sounds like they are trying to out-drink each other. *I don't know how they can fit all that liquid into their body after eating Grandma's big dinner.*

Aunt May is getting pretty mad at Uncle Jimmy. He is even slurring his words now.

"Why don't ya go in and get me 'nother beer, May?"

"I don't think you need anymore beer, Jimmy. You can hardly walk now!"

"I'm not drunk. I'm just tired. Please?"

"Okay, but this is your last beer, and then you need to do some sobering up for the drive home."

Grandma and Mama go inside with Aunt May to bring out beer for everyone. There are beer bottles all over the yard. Roy says he is going to line those bottles up on the fence by the pasture and get some target practice in tomorrow.

"Jimmy, you still want your massage, Hun?"

"Sure do, sweet thing. But you better do it before May comes back, or she'll have both our hides!"

"Yeah, and when you're done givin' old Jim here a massage, I can use 'nother one!" Uncle Frank says to Caroline, slurring his words.

"Frank, you doll, how could I forget you? It will be my pleasure to massage you again, Hun!"

When Mama and Aunt May arrive outside, Caroline is just finishing up with Uncle Jimmy's massage. Uncle Jimmy has the biggest grin on his face I ever did see.

"Caroline, honey, my shoulders still hurt. Where's my massage? You said you would give me another massage after you finished Jimmy's!"

"There's no need for Caroline to give anyone a massage, especially you, Frank. You drunk S.O.B! And, Caroline, you are nothing but a slut! You always cause trouble! Why don't you just leave?" Mama screams at both of them.

"Papa, are you going to let Dot talk to me like this?"

"What's the matter, Caroline, does the truth hurt? You better keep your dirty hands off Jimmy, or you'll find yourself eating dirt!" Aunt May tells Caroline, gritting her teeth.

"Caroline isn't doing anything wrong, Dot. She is only trying to release the tension in my shoulders. Which is more than I can say you do for me nowadays," Uncle Frank tells Mama, tripping over a beer bottle as he tries to stand. "And what about you kissing and dancing with Roger? You said you were just friends!"

"That's the way to tell her, Frank!" Roy hollers.

"Frank, I should have killed you when I had the chance. You'll never learn to keep your big fat mouth shut. Roger was a much better man than you'll ever be!" Mama yells, as she smacks him in the face.

"Ow…Dot, that hurt! You touch me again and I'll kill you…just like…never mind."

"Don't you ever threaten me again you cheap bastard. Be glad it is my hand instead of one of those bottles of beer you're guzzling! "

Roy grabs an empty beer bottle and raises his hand. "I think the only people who better leave and get the hell off my property are you two. I want you two to leave now before I knock you both out myself. You won't have to worry about any old massage Caroline gives your men!"

"You think so, old man!" Mama taunts Roy.

"Irene, you better tell your sorry ass daughters to leave now, before I do something. I don't want to look at them another minute. They better never call my daughter a slut again on my property or anywhere else. Do you hear me, old woman?"

"Roy, calm down. There's no need for any yelling or name calling. Let's all be sensible adults here!"

Aunt May begins crying. "Mother, the only thing that would be sensible is for you to leave that hateful man!"

"That's it. You girls get your brood and get the hell off my property now!"

"Frank, you find your own way home. You're not riding back with us! Come on kids, get your stuff; we're leaving this awful man's property. Sorry, Mother, we didn't mean to ruin your birthday."

"Jimmy, get the kids in the car, now! We're going home and we're never coming back here till Roy's gone!"

"You don't mean it, May. It's the liquor talking!"

"But I do, Mother. I'm sorry. And I'm sorry Caroline is here to ruin your birthday!"

Caroline puts her arm around Frank's neck. "I'll take you home, Frank. You don't have to worry about little old Dot, honey. She doesn't scare me!" She glares at Mama.

"Go on about your business, Dot. You worry about getting your brood and getting off my property. Caroline and I will take good care of Frank!" Roy tells Mama.

"Hey, Dot, 'member what happened to your kid's daddy. If you don't want them to lose their mama, ya better watch what ya do!"

We all get into Mama's old car and drive home without Uncle Frank. Maybe, if we're lucky, Caroline will want to keep Uncle Frank forever. For a minute, I think I am riding in a boat as much as Mama is swerving our car. It is a good thing there aren't many cars on the back roads tonight or we might meet them head-on. And Uncle Frank might just get his wish, unless we kids all die, too!

The next day, Grandma Irene brings Uncle Frank home. I never did hear if Caroline took good care of Uncle Frank. I don't know if Mama and Uncle Frank even know what they fought about. Katie and I remember every word!

Chapter Fifteen

Mama and Uncle Frank don't sleep in the same room when he comes back home. Mama makes him a bed on a cot in our study. The cot sure doesn't look comfortable. Uncle Frank keeps telling Mama he needs Caroline around for a massage. This really makes her angry. We know they are going to have words. Katie and I listen through the register to make sure no one uses the rolling pin this time.

"Frank, you're going to sleep on the cot until hell freezes over, or until you move out. I don't want anything more to do with your sorry ass. My mother told me you slept in her spare bedroom with Caroline after I left. There is nothing you can say or do that will change my mind!"

"I was drunk. I don't remember what happened!"

"Oh, don't start, Frank. Don't you even think you're going to use alcohol as an excuse this time. I have witnesses!"

"But Caroline seduced me."

"You are such a liar! You were flirting with her from the

moment she arrived at Mother's. What's wrong with you men? The minute Caroline walks into a room you all lose your head."

"What would you do if I slept with some other man, Frank? You would leave me in a minute. You're jealous if I even talk to another man. You even threatened to kill Roger if you saw him giving me a peck on the cheek. Did you have something to do with his accident? Furthermore, you keep bringing up Dan's accident. If I didn't know his death was accidental, I'd think you had something to do with it. You need to find another place to live. I don't want to hear any more lies or excuses!"

"Dot, I love you. It was only one night. Please forgive me? I promise I won't even look at another woman. You're all I ever want. If I can't have you, I'll make sure no one else will either!"

"I have to get ready for work. I don't have time to argue. This conversation is over!"

When Katie and I hear it is over between Mama and Uncle Frank, we want to go up on top of our flat garage and scream, "Hallelujah."

"I sure hope Mama means it this time, Missy. I can't stand the thought of Uncle Frank in our house any longer!"

"He frightens me, Katie. If looks could kill, we'd all be dead by now!"

Katie shivers. "He frightens me, too. I'm not sure Daddy's—I'm not sure he hasn't made good on some of his threats. It's too bad he can't go share a place with Uncle Sammy. Those two are a lot alike!"

I can't wait to get downstairs. It is so hot up in our bedroom you can fry an egg on my window sill. A glass of Mama's fresh lemonade sure sounds refreshing. If we are lucky, Uncle Frank will be gone by the time we reach the kitchen.

"You look real nice tonight, Mama. Is there something special going on at the Victory Bar & Grill?" Katie asks.

Mama stands in front of a mirror above the kitchen sink applying mascara. "No, darling, your Mama just wants to make herself feel proud of who she is. Tonight is going to be a new beginning for us. I feel better about myself than I have in a very long time!"

"How long do you think Uncle Frank is going to continue living here, Mama?" Katie asks concerned.

"One day is too long. We'll see what comes our way!"

"Katie, make grilled cheese and tomato soup for supper. Don't forget to have a couple of my dill pickles, too. I'll be home around two in the morning. Don't you kids wait up for me. And don't let Frank boss you around, ya hear. He's not your old Uncle Frank anymore. You can just call him, Frank!"

Sandy starts barking as soon as Mama leaves. "You can't go with Mama right now. Stop barking! Come on, girl. You want me to play ball with you? It's okay, Sandy, I miss Mama when she's working, too."

Katie puts her hand on Billie's shoulder. "How about we go ride our bikes, Billie? Sandy can even come with us."

"That's a deal! Riding bikes always makes me hungry. Then we'll really be hungry for supper after riding, won't we, Katie?"

"Sure will! Do you want to help me make the grilled cheese?"

"Oh boy, do I? Do I get to flip the sandwich in the pan?"

Katie laughs. "Yes, Billie. I'll even let you flip the grilled cheese."

"This is even better than Mama being home. She sure wouldn't let me cook those sandwiches. She would just tell me I'm still too little. You're the best sister a boy could ever have!"

"Hey, what about me?"

"I guess you're special too!" He says, giving me a hug.

"Hey, Katie, do you think we can have a race on the big hill by the school?"

"I guess."

"That's not fair, Katie. I have to ride that old boy's bike Mama bought at a garage sale. You know I will lose!"

"It's no big deal, Missy. Just let Billie win. Mama and Uncle Frank fighting is upsetting to him. He's too little to under-stand what is happening between them."

"Billie might be too little, but I don't have to call Frank, Uncle Frank any longer. Mama said so. And you don't have to call him Uncle Frank either!"

"Okay, go get your bikes. Let's get this race on the road. Come on Sandy, you ready girl?" Katie asks her.

Sandy just stands by Katie's side waiting for Billie and me. She loves to tag along anywhere we go.

"This seat is hard on my butt, Katie. Can we trade bikes?" I ask, my butt already aching.

"Not on your life. I bought this bike with my babysitting money!"

"It's not fair. This bike is meant for a boy, not a girl. I'm too short for this old bike. And the bar hurts my butt when I get on and off!" I complain even louder this time.

"Just deal with it you big baby or you can stay home with Frank by yourself!"

"No thanks. I'm coming with you guys!"

Sandy and Katie arrive at the hill first, with Billie close behind. I am about half a block behind and out of breath.

Katie makes a starting line on the top of the hill. We all have to stay behind the line until someone says the word "go".

"Can I count to three, please?"

Katie winks at me. "Okay, Billie."

I still don't see how it's fair I have to let Billie win. If I win fair and square, then I should be able to declare myself the winner.

"One...two...three...go!" Billie yells.

The hill is as long as a block and about as steep as a mountain. It makes for great sledding in the winter. But if you are riding bikes, you only want to ride up it once. You don't even have to pedal on the way down, you can just glide.

Halfway down my pant leg gets caught in the spokes. "Help, Katie, my pants are caught!" *It is a long way to the bottom of this hill.* "I'm going to fall!"

My bike falls over with me on top, just rolling down that steep hill. "Ow...ow...ow...." I begin crying. I can't help myself. It hurts. "Katie, I'm bleeding and my left side has no skin on it. I don't think I can move. Ow...ow...I want Mama!"

"Good Lord, Missy! You're going to live. Stop your crying. The whole neighborhood is going to hear you."

"But it hurts!"

Billie already reached the bottom of the hill. "I won. I won!"

"You did not. I fell!"

"I won, didn't I, Katie? It's Missy's fault she couldn't stay on that old boy's bike"

"Yes. You sure did win!"

Katie is better with little kids than me. That's why all the neighbors want her to baby-sit. *I wouldn't have let him think he won. He has to learn how to lose someday.*

Sandy comes over to me and starts licking my tears. At least she still loves me and cares about me.

"Katie, I think I broke something. Look at all the blood oozing through my pants. They are ruined. Mama's going to be real mad!"

"Mama's not going to be mad at you, Missy. Stand up and try to walk!"

The top of my pants are soaked and are now stuck to my shredded flesh "Ow…ow…it hurts too much to walk!"

"Billie, give me your shirt. I need it to wipe off some of Missy's blood."

"Okay, but you tell Mama where my shirt went, I'm not!"

"Ow…Katie, don't touch it. It hurts!"

"I don't think anything is broken, but there sure isn't any skin left on your side."

"I can't walk. How am I supposed to get home?"

"Now you hear me, Missy Canfield. You are picking your bike up and walking it home. No one else is going to do it for you. You will live!"

"I sure wish Mama was here," I cry. "She would go get her car and drive me home!"

"Well I don't have a car, do I?"

I knew there was a reason I didn't want to ride this darn boy's bike anywhere. I wouldn't have got my pants stuck in a girl's bike. If the bar hadn't been there, I could have just jumped off. I wouldn't have fallen so hard and hurt my side either.

Billie bends down close. "Your side looks real neat. Maybe Mama will take a picture of it!"

"That's not funny! You wouldn't think it was so neat if it was your bloody side and had no skin!"

When we get home, Katie helps me out of my torn clothes. She takes some warm rags and gently washes my open wound.

"Stand in the tub, Missy. I'm going to pour some warm water down your side. You might want to hold on to the towel bar so you don't slip."

"Katie, it hurts real bad!"

"It looks like there's some pieces of gravel stuck in your side. I have to try and get the gravel out."

"No! Just leave it alone. Please, Katie?"

"Missy, Mama can't afford a doctor if you get an infection, and she sure can't afford to miss any work. I called her and she told me what to do. Now, just hold your breath. I'm going to use Mama's tweezers and pull the gravel out."

"Ow...ow...haven't you got it all yet?"

"Katie, can I come in and watch you take the gravel out of Missy's side?" Billie asks.

"No, she doesn't have any clothes on and she doesn't need you to watch her cry!"

"Boy, I never get to have any fun."

"Go outside and play with your army men until we're done, Billie. Then you can help cook Missy's grilled cheese."

"Missy, I think I only see one...more...piece...of gravel and we're done. Do you think you can stand still long enough for me to get it?"

"That better be all!"

If Katie or Billie had hurt their side as I hurt mine, I don't think they would be standing still either. If fact, they would both probably be crying more than I am!

"That's all I see, Missy. Hold on. I've...got it. We're done!"

"I'll wet one of Mama's dishtowels with warm water and you can keep putting the warm towel on your side."

"I don't want anything touching my side. That includes a dishtowel, Katie!"

"What am I going to put on for clothes? My pants will rub on my side."

"Go put on one of your cotton nightgowns and rest on the couch. I'll bring you a Bobbsey Twins book to read while Billie and I make your dinner. Do you want an aspirin? I think Mama would give you one if she were here."

"Okay, maybe it will help with the pain. Thanks, Katie!"

After I take the aspirin, I fall asleep on the couch. I don't even finish two pages of my book. I dreamt I was flying through the air and every time I tried touching the ground, I landed on my side. Mama tries to catch me a few times, but I just bounce right over her head. I remember telling Mama, "Look at me. I'm flying!"

Billie whispers. "Missy, your dinner's done. Wake up. I cooked your grilled cheese all by myself. I brought you a tray and everything just like in the hospital. Wake up and eat it before it gets cold."

"Hmm...I'm awake, Billie. It sure does smell good." I try sitting up but my side is stuck to the warm rag which is now cold, and I don't want my clothes to touching my side. "You'll have to wait a minute; it might take a few tries before I can sit up without hurting my side more."

"Are you ready for your tray now, Missy?" Billie asks me.

"I'm as ready as I'll ever be."

"It's going to be the best grilled cheese you ever ate!"

"Maybe it will, Billie."

"How is your side?" Katie asks.

"It hurts a lot!"

"Mama will look at it when she gets home."

Katie and Billie are trying to take good care of me. I almost don't miss Mama. Billie's grilled cheese looks real good. I couldn't have cooked it better myself. It isn't even burnt.

We hear Frank's car pull up in the driveway. We know it won't be long before he comes in the house and asks questions about Mama. Maybe he won't be drunk this time.

Frank comes in the house and walks over to the stove to see what Katie's cooking.

"Where's my grilled cheese, Katie?"

"I didn't cook you one. You weren't home and Mama said you can cook your own food!" Frank throws the frying pan in the sink, making a loud noise. Then he opens the refrigerator and grabs a bottle of cold beer.

He takes his beer and storms out of the house slamming the screen door behind him. Pretty soon we hear Sandy yelp.

"Stay out of my way!"

Billie runs to the screen door and retrieves Sandy, showing old Frank his fist. "Don't you ever kick my dog again, Frank!" Billie runs out the door screaming at him; showing him his fist.

"Billie, you get in this house with Sandy right now, young man. Leave Frank alone before he kicks you next!" Katie warns him.

Billie holds his fists up ready for a fight. "I ought to kick the prune juice right out of that old weasel!"

"Billie Canfield, I don't want to ever hear you talk like that again. Frank might hear you and do more than kick you!" Katie warns him again.

"Where do you think Frank's going, Katie?" Billie asks.

"I don't know and I don't care! Just eat your food while it's still warm."

"Billie, this is the best grilled cheese I've ever tasted!" I tell him, hoping he forgets about old Frank.

"Can I get you anything else, Missy?"

"Thanks. I sure could use another aspirin for the pain if we have any."

Billie marches into the kitchen with Sandy at his side. I think she knows he isn't going to let anyone hurt his dog.

Katie and Billie do the dishes as I lie on the couch. Sandy is lying by my feet as if to say she's sorry I'm hurt. I read some of my Bobbsey Twins book to Sandy; she rather enjoys the attention.

"Want to play cards, Missy?" Billie asks. "It might make you feel better!"

Katie winks at me.

"I suppose it won't hurt my side too much, Billie. I guess I can play cards for a while."

Frank comes back home drunk about midnight. He doesn't look happy. I know we better stay out of his way.

"Where's that mother of yours?"

"Frank, it's only midnight and you know Mama works till one or two in the morning," Katie tells him.

"What is this Frank stuff, with you kids? What happened to Uncle Frank?"

Katie, Billie, and I look at each other not sure of what to tell him or how he might respond.

Katie begins shaking. "Uhh—Mama told us to call you Frank from now on. You'll have to ask her what her reason is."

"You tell that tramp to wake me up when she gets home. I want to talk to her!"

Frank stumbles off to the study to pass out on his cot. I don't think he's going to be doing much talking to anyone soon. He won't even remember what he said to us by tomorrow.

"Katie, are you going to tell Mama what Frank called her?" Billie asks.

"Uhh—I think we need for Mama to look at Missy's side. That's more important now. And Mama doesn't need anymore trouble with Frank. But, Billie, try to stay out of Frank's way while he's still living here. Don't go following him out the door yelling at him again. This means you, too, Missy. And whatever you do, keep Sandy out of his way."

I really am not into playing cards after Frank comes home. I don't think Katie is either, but we play them to keep Billie entertained.

"I must be getting better at playing rummy, Missy. I beat you the last two games! Do you think it's harder to beat me now?"

"I think you've got the best teachers in the world right here, Billie. We've taught you everything we know. Now you're beating us," I tell him.

"You feel like playing Monopoly next?"

"No, Billie, you know I lose every time. Besides, Mama will be home soon."

"I sure hope Mama and Frank don't fight tonight, I'm tired."

Katie pipes up. "Billie, Frank's too drunk and he's probably passed out by now. He won't hear a thing the rest of the night. You don't have to worry about them fighting tonight, unless you tell Mama what Frank said."

"I won't, I promise!"

"Why don't you get your pajamas on and go to bed. I'm going to wait up for Mama with Missy so she can take a look at her side."

"Okay, I'm tired anyway. Can I sleep with Sandy?"

"I think that's a good idea, especially if Frank wakes up."

Mama arrives home later than usual. It is about three in the morning. Katie and I have fallen asleep on the couch. She is sure bubbly and talking up a streak. We can hardly get a word in.

"Where's Frank, Katie?"

"He's passed out in the study, Mama. I don't think you want to wake him!"

"How are you feeling, Missy?"

"My side really hurts, Mama. Katie cleaned up the wound and took all the gravel out with your tweezers. I don't think you need to touch it!" I sure hope Mama doesn't touch my side. It has been touched enough by Katie already. *I don't know if I can stand any more pain. I might just pass out this time.*

"Remind me tomorrow to clean my tweezers, Katie. I hope you cleaned them good before you used them on Missy."

"I did, Mama. I put the tweezers in a pan of boiling water to sterilize them before I used them."

I turn over and pretend to go back to sleep; hoping Mama will leave me alone for at least tonight.

"Missy, you're not going to get off that easy. Let's go in the kitchen where there is more light. I need to take a look at your side!"

"Don't touch it, Mama! Please?" I beg.

"Missy, we don't want you to get an infection. Let me take a look at it!"

"Okay, but...be gentle."

I take off my nightgown so Mama can see my side. I sure hope Frank is passed out and doesn't come in the kitchen. He still seems as perverted as Uncle Sammy.

"Missy, Katie's right. You don't have any skin left on your side. We are going to have to put some mercurochrome on it"

"No…Mama, that stuff stings! Please?" I cry.

"Missy, keep it down. Remember, we don't want to wake Frank!"

"Okay, I'll try. Katie, will you hold my hand?"

"Sure, I know how bad that stuff stings."

"Ow…Mama…ow…that burns! Don't put any more mercurochrome on my side! Please?" I say, trying not to scream.

Mama gives me a kiss on my cheek. "My poor baby, I'm sorry you had to walk your bike home all the way with your side like this. You sure are brave!"

She gives Katie a kiss on her cheek, too. "Katie, you did a good job of taking care of your sister today. I'm really proud of you. I guess you are growing up to be a fine young lady!"

Katie's eyes light up like a Christmas tree when Mama tells her she is proud of her. *I think Katie feels pretty important. And she is! She took care of me as good as Mama ever has.*

Chapter Sixteen

Frank leaves the house before Mama wakes up. Maybe if we are lucky he is out looking for another place to live. Mama sleeps in peacefully for once.

Mama finally comes out of her bedroom. "Ah—it feels so good to have my bed all to myself!"

"Is Frank still here?"

"No, Mama," I tell her. "He left awhile ago."

"Thank goodness. I hope he never comes back! Did he take any clothes with him?"

"No. He just left the same as usual wearing a white shirt."

"How about I make you kids some biscuits and sausage gravy for breakfast?"

"That sounds yummy!" Billie shouts excited.

It is one of his favorite meals. Mama hasn't made biscuits and gravy since Frank and Sammy came to live with us. They always want pancakes, eggs, sausage, and hash browns for breakfast when they are home.

"Can I help you make breakfast, Mama?" Katie asks.

"Sure, it's about time you learned how to make milk gravy anyway."

Mama makes the best milk gravy in the whole world. It is one of Dixon Inn's specials every morning. Mama told us kids that the men come into the restaurant bringing their wives saying, "Now honey, ask Dot how to make her biscuits and sausage gravy so you can make it for me at home." Mama says she always gives them her recipe, but those men just keep coming back insisting she didn't give them the whole thing.

They ask her, "Dot, you sure you wrote down the whole recipe for my wife?" Mama says those men coming in and complaining their wives can't cook like her makes her feel special.

Mama doesn't have to work today. We have the pleasure of her cooking breakfast for us instead of her customers. I almost feel sorry for her customers when she isn't cooking. Their other cooks can't cook as well as she can.

"I'm going to go fishing with Aunt May when I'm done making breakfast. You kids stay close to home."

"Mama, can I go, too?" Billie asks excited.

"No, Billie, Aunt May wants some time without kids tagging along. You know how she needs time away. Besides, she wants to talk to me about something real important in private!"

"Okay, Mama, but if you change your mind I can be ready

real fast."

Laughing, Mama tells Billie, "If I change my mind, you'll be the first to know. Katie, I should be back by suppertime if anyone asks. If we're lucky, we'll eat catfish tonight for supper."

I don't think that is what Katie wants to hear from Mama. She hates eating fish and the smell makes her sick.

"Mama, I don't know anyone as lucky as you are at fishing except Uncle Jimmy!"

"Thanks, Katie. If you have time, you can peel and slice some potatoes for supper. Remember to put them in a bowl of cold water so they don't turn brown."

"I will, Mama. And, Mama is Frank eating supper with us tonight?"

"We'll have to just wait and see. I don't know what his plans are."

Mama gets dressed up real pretty for fishing today. I hope she doesn't tangle her fishing line and fall in.

"Katie, why do you think Mama got so dressed up to go fishing? I've never seen her look like that when she fishes with me," I comment.

"Maybe her having so many new clothes from Frank and Uncle Riley means she doesn't need somewhere special to wear them all, Missy."

"That's probably true. Don't you wish we had that many clothes, too?"

"Not if I have to sleep with Frank to get them!" Katie says

disgusted.

"Sandy, what are you barking at, girl?" Katie asks her.

Pretty soon we hear the garage door open.

Smiling and carrying packages, Frank asks Katie, "Where's Dot, I have a surprise for her!"

"Mama's not home right now, Frank. She said she will be home in time for supper."

"I thought she has the day off."

"She did. She went fishing with Aunt May."

"During the week, isn't that unusual? Why didn't she take you kids with or at least Billie? She always takes him with her fishing."

"Mama said Aunt May wants to talk to her about something private, Frank. You're just going to have to wait and ask Mama those questions. She doesn't tell us everything she does. She is an adult, and we're just kids!"

"You're getting a little too smart for your own good, Katie. I'm going to have to put you in your place one of these days. God, how I hate smart aleck kids. And stop calling me Frank. I'm, Uncle Frank, to you."

Frank goes to Mama's bedroom carrying his packages. He stays in her room for a long time.

"Katie, why do you think Frank keeps buying Mama presents?" I ask confused.

"Well, Missy, I think he's trying to buy Mama's love but it

isn't working."

Still puzzled, I say, "I thought Mama told Frank to move out."

"She did. I don't think Frank buying Mama presents is going to help him stick around this time!"

Katie whispers to Billie and me. "Let's go outside and play cards until Mama gets home. I don't think we should be inside with Frank right now. He seems different lately, like he's not all there!"

"Come on, Sandy, you better come outside with us, too. Frank just might kick you again." I tell her, worried Frank is going to injure her one of these days.

Sandy is always happy whenever anyone, except Frank, talks to her. She just wags her little tail forever.

I wish we didn't have to sit outside. It is sure hot. I don't know how Mama and Aunt May are going to catch any fish. Mama has a better chance than Aunt May. If anyone can catch a fish today, it will be Mama using her vanilla.

Just as Mama said she would, she arrives home with catfish wrapped in brown paper at suppertime. She has already skinned and cleaned the catfish.

"Mama, I thought I would get to help you clean those catfish!" Billie cries.

"When I took Aunt May home, we cleaned them at her house."

"Darn, I bet Bobby got to help you clean those fish!"

"No, Billie, he was off playing somewhere and I didn't even see him or Rita. No one helped Aunt May and me clean our fish," Mama tells him, giving him a great big kiss.

"Katie, where's Frank?"

"He was in your bedroom the last time any of us saw him."

"What was he doing in my room? I told him to move out!"

We all just shrug our shoulders. We sure can't keep track of what Frank does. For that matter, we can't keep track of what Mama does either. It really is too bad we didn't just bury him in our compost heap out back. Then we wouldn't have to worry about him moving out or fighting with Mama. And we wouldn't have to answer questions about where either one of them are.

Mama sets the catfish down on the kitchen counter. Then she storms off to her room to confront Frank. We just know there will be another fight soon. *I hope we got to eat our supper first, I am hungry.*

Mama comes out of her bedroom wearing a brand new outfit.

She whirls around showing off her new yellow dress. "Kids, look what Frank bought me! Isn't this wonderful?"

"Mama, the dress is really pretty, especially on you," Katie tells her.

"Don't sound so sad. Does it really look that bad on me?"

"No, Mama, how can anything look bad on you? You always look beautiful no matter what you wear!"

"It's a shame I have to take this dress off to cook those darn catfish. I sure wouldn't want it smelling like the river and I sure don't want grease splattering all over it. You, kids, set the table and don't forget to set a place for Frank. I'm going to change."

Frank peeks through the door to the kitchen. He just gives us kids his big evil grin. We all know Frank will be around for a few more days. Mama needs to stop accepting Frank's presents every time they have a fight. When is she ever going to learn? The first time one of them has a drink or she looks at a man, they will be fighting again. *When I say my prayers, I am just going to have to ask God why he keeps sending that evil man back to us!*

"Dot, these catfish sure taste good. You and May must have caught a lot of fish today for us to have this many to eat!"

Mama winks at us kids. "You know me. I can catch anything using vanilla. And Rita and Bobby weren't going to be home for supper tonight so May gave me most of her fish."

Our supper sure tasted good. We had catfish, fried potatoes, corn muffins and ears of sweet corn for supper. The only drawback; there will be plenty of dishes for us to wash later. As usual, Katie didn't eat the fish but this time, she won't be able to get out of doing the dishes.

At bedtime, we hear Mama and Frank screaming at each other. I try putting a couch pillow over my head, but I can't drown out what they're screaming.

"How come those kids of yours are calling me Frank?"

"I told them you are moving out, and they don't need to call you Uncle Frank anymore I also told you to sleep in the study. You're not moving back into my bedroom now or ever!"

"But, Dot, I bought you those new clothes, and we had supper together just like normal."

"You being in this house isn't normal. And sleeping with some slut sure wasn't going to get you back in my bedroom!"

"You're going to regret telling me to leave. You might just end up like that no good friend of yours, Roger. It really was convenient for Dan to die so I could have you. You know, Dot, if I can't have you, no other man is going to have you either. I'll make sure of it!"

Frank comes out of Mama's bedroom slamming the door. He goes to the study and brings out a suitcase.

"What are you kids staring at? Aren't you supposed to be in bed by now?" He says, not waiting for an answer; slamming the garage door on his way out.

Mama comes out of her bedroom next with her hair all messed up. Her face is beet read and her mascara is running.

Katie walks over to Mama and gives her a kiss on the cheek. "Are you okay, Mama?"

"That depends if Frank moves out!"

"Why do you stay with him, Mama? He scares us! He keeps threatening to kill you. You almost killed him! And why does he keep bringing up Daddy's accident?"

Mama begins picking at her bright red fingernails. "Frank's just blowing off steam. He's just trying to make himself look big. He won't be around much longer. I promise!"

"Mama, maybe today's our lucky day. Frank took his suitcase when he left!"

"I wouldn't count on us being that lucky. Frank's like a bad dream, he just keeps reappearing nightly."

The next morning when we get up, Sandy comes to my bedroom window and begins barking. When Katie and I look out, we see Frank sleeping in our hammock close to Mama's bedroom window in his boxer shorts.

"Oh, no, what if the neighbors see Frank like this. I'll never live it down!" Katie says, humiliated by the scene she is witnessing.

"We'd better go and tell Mama, Katie. I don't think she's going to be happy with Frank. She thought he moved out for good this time."

"Come on, Sandy, let's go tell Mama." I say, following Katie to Mama's bedroom.

"Mama, Frank's sleeping outside your window on our hammock in his underwear!" I say, trying to wake her.

Mama yawns and then bolts upright. "He's what? You're kidding me! I thought he didn't come home last night."

We leave Mama alone to get dressed. I thought for sure she was going to jump out the bedroom window to smack old

Frank.

"Oh, Missy, the kids already tease me about having two men living here. Now, what are they going to say?" Katie says in tears, covering her face.

"Maybe Mama will get him in the house before anyone else sees him. It is still early."

Katie wipes her face on the sleeve of her robe. "Oh, let's hope so, Missy!"

It isn't long before we hear Mama screaming at Frank. He tells her he isn't going to let another man sleep in her bed. He moved the hammock outside her window to make sure of that. It was hot out there last night so he took his clothes off to cool off.

Sandy's barking gets louder the more Frank and Mama argue. We try getting her to come in the house with us but she won't leave Mama's side. She's making sure Frank doesn't touch her.

"Why don't you get rid of your dog, Dot? She's not good for anything except barking. She needs to go to the pound and be put to sleep. If you can't do it, I'll do it for you!"

"Don't you talk about my dog like that, Frank Billings. She's not going anywhere. You are!"

Frank kicks Sandy's side. "Like hell, I am!"

Sandy being kicked by old Frank makes her mad. She goes straight for Frank's bare feet and tries biting them. The more he kicks at her the madder she gets.

"Ow, you damn dog. Don't you ever bite me again!"

"Leave my dog alone, Frank!"

"Come on, Sandy. Let's go in the house. Having you is much better than having any man around!" Mama tells her dog.

Old Frank must have seen the neighbors staring over the fence. He turns his back and puts his clothes on. The next thing we hear is his car screeching down the road.

Frank is gone for a couple of days. Mama seems really happy. She is smiling and singing country western songs to the radio just like old times. She will just be singing and Sandy will be howling along.

She takes Billie fishing by himself. He is so happy to have all her attention. They pack a picnic basket full of Billie's favorite foods. When they return home, Mama even lets him help clean their fish.

Katie sits out on a quilt reading a book while trying to get her tan back. It has been a while since either of us has felt safe enough to wear a bathing suit in our back yard. Now, with Frank and Sammy gone, we both feel more relaxed.

I just sit in the shade and read my books. Once in awhile I take a break and try drawing our red barn with apple trees in front of it. *It sure is peaceful without Frank and Mama fighting. Mama doesn't need any man around, she has us. And she already told Sandy she is better than any old man.*

Frank finally shows up on our doorsteps again a couple of

days later; bringing Mama more gifts. This time he even brings Mama a pearl ring. It has the biggest pearl on top of a gold band I have ever seen. He tells her the ring is as pure as their love. *Yuck!*

Mama still makes him sleep in the study. She doesn't know who he has been sleeping with while he was gone. Who knows, he might have been staying with Caroline again. He says he stayed with Sammy, but I don't think Mama believes him.

On Mama's next day off and after Frank leaves for work, she tells us she is going fishing again with Aunt May. *What is so important Aunt May has to talk to Mama in private?* Maybe she and Uncle Jimmy aren't getting along. He was flirting with Caroline a lot at Grandma Irene's birthday party. Maybe they got into a fight over Caroline just like Mama and Frank did. I will have to ask Rita and Bobby the next time I see them.

Mama actually beats Frank home. She has supper ready when he walks through the door. We are eating catfish again. No one set a place for Frank at the table. We didn't know if he would be home today or if he moved out again.

"Katie, set a place at the table for Frank."

"No need, Dot. I already ate. I see you're having catfish again. Is this starting a tradition on your day off? To go fishing and have catfish for supper?"

"We are hungry, and our supper is done. If you don't have anything nice to say, you can leave while we eat!"

Frank stomps into the next room. The rest of our meal is

pleasant and peaceful. Mama doesn't let Frank get to her. She is in a really good mood.

Mama and Frank don't argue. He just stays in the study all night long. We even talk Mama into playing rummy with us. She seems happier than she has in months despite the fact she loses every game of rummy and old Frank is in the study.

It isn't like Frank to stay in his room. He isn't even picking a fight with Mama. Maybe he is sick or maybe he found a new place to live while he was gone and is packing. Tomorrow is a new day, anything can happen with Frank still around.

When I wake up, there are two red finches outside my bedroom. The sun is beating through the lace curtains. I just want to lie in bed and read one of my books from our study.

"Kids, wake up and throw down your dirty laundry. It's a beautiful day to hang the laundry outside."

I don't know how any day can be a beautiful day to do work, especially laundry. Laundry means Katie and I will be spending the entire afternoon ironing. This includes ironing Frank's boxer shorts!

We hear Mama knocking on the door to the study to wake Frank. At least we know he didn't sleep in her room last night. Maybe there is hope of him moving out yet.

"Frank, throw out your dirty laundry. I'm going to do the wash."

"You sure you want to do my laundry?"

"I don't want those smelly socks of yours stinking up my new study!"

Katie and I get a tickle out of Mama telling Frank his feet

stink. We wanted to tell him that many times before. I sure don't want my books smelling like his feet.

Mama drinks coffee while sorting out the laundry in the kitchen. She is singing and dancing along with the radio. She seems happy until we hear a scream come out of her like some horror flick.

"Frank, you sorry bastard; get in this kitchen!"

"What's your problem now?"

"Who have you been sleeping with this time?"

"No one. I promise. I have been in the study by myself!"

"Since when did you start wearing pink lipstick?"

"Now, Dot, give me a break. I am hard up, but I wouldn't resort to wearing lipstick of any color. The last I looked I was still a man even though I haven't been able to use my tools lately!"

"Then whose lipsticks do you suppose is on the collar of this white shirt?"

Mama holds up Frank's white shirt so close to his eyes I think he is going to be wearing it on his face soon.

"Dot, it must be yours! You're the only person I've been with since I slept with Caroline."

"Caroline wouldn't wear pink lipstick either. So who is it, Frank?"

"It must have rubbed off of some waitress when she served me my food!"

"Funny, Frank! When I serve my customers, I never get lipstick on their collar. I have heard better lies from ten-year-olds. Try again. Better yet, just get out of my sight. I take that back. Get the hell out of my house. I want you out today or I'm having Riley come and throw you and your stuff out!"

"Dot, you don't mean it." Frank whines.

"Try me. I'll have him here in twenty minutes!"

"Don't you go calling Riley. He's been questioning me enough lately. Just give me a few days to find another place first!"

Mama goes through her laundry basket and throws Frank's laundry in his face. "Do your own damn laundry from now on. And, Frank, what have you done that Riley's questioning you?"

"As if you don't know. Riley still has a thing for you!"

Mama looks at Frank and smiles. *If we are lucky, she still has a thing for him, too.*

Us kids get a tickle out of Mama throwing Frank's dirty underwear in his face.

"What are you brats looking at? You probably put the pink lipstick on my collar to get me into trouble with your Ma. You are always causing us trouble. Do you have any pink lipstick, Katie?"

"Frank, I don't ever want to hear you talking to my kids like that again. You got yourself into trouble; no one else did that for you. Katie wouldn't put lipstick on your shirt. Stop making excuses. No one here believes you anymore. Now get out!"

Frank doesn't come home for supper. Mama makes us liver and onions and mashed potatoes with onion gravy for supper. Katie doesn't care much for meat, especially liver. She makes herself a grilled cheese and onion sandwich. Mama always says just because liver is real cheap it doesn't mean it has to taste bad. When Frank is home, he doesn't even let Mama have beef liver in the house. He says liver is for fish bait. We only use chicken liver for our bait, not beef liver. Besides, Mama says liver is supposed to be good for you!

Mama has to work at the Varsity Bar & Grill tonight until two. She looks a little worried about leaving us home. We are a little worried about her leaving us home alone, too!

"Now kids, if Frank comes back, I want you to stay away from him. Whatever you do, don't make him mad. Billie, you keep Sandy in your room tonight!"

Frank returns around midnight. He is so drunk he can hardly walk. After he goes in the bathroom and throws up all over the floor, he goes straight to the study.

"Katie, shouldn't Frank clean up his own puke?" Billie asks.

"Billie, Mama said not to make Frank mad. You know how he gets when he's been drinking. I'll just have to clean it up before Mama gets home. We don't need those two fighting tonight!"

Billie takes Sandy to bed with him. He doesn't want her anywhere near Frank. Katie and I stay up talking in our bedroom. We can't figure out why Mama and Aunt May are fishing together so much during the day. And we both are sick of cleaning up the smelly dishes from the catfish.

Mama comes home around three in the morning. She must have had a lot of customers to clean up after to be home so late. It is a good thing Frank is already passed out in the study.

The next morning, we kids sleep in. We don't even hear Mama or Frank leave for work. When we wake, we find a note taped to my dresser.

Kids,

I am going fishing after cooking at Dixon Inn today. Aunt May is going to meet me at the river. Make yourself some bologna sandwiches for lunch and whatever you can find for supper. Don't tell Frank where I'm at. Stay out of his way, and don't argue with him.

See you later tonight. Be good. Hugs and kisses.

Love,

Mama

"Missy, I wonder if Aunt May is pregnant with twins again. Mama said she was really stressed out during that pregnancy and Aunt May wanted her by her side every spare minute. I know she sure wouldn't want to be pregnant again, especially with twins!"

"Well come to think of it, Katie, Aunt May does look like

her stomach is getting bigger like Calico's did!"

"Yeah, maybe that's it," Katie and I agree.

"Katie, how come Mama and Aunt May can't take me with? I can fish while they talk. I don't mind!" Billie says.

"Well, Billie, you sure can fish, but you've never been good at keeping secrets," Katie laughs. "How about we get Missy's red wagon and go around town and collect soda pop bottles. Then maybe we can go buy you a new comic book with the deposit money."

"That's a deal!"

We get my red wagon and happily go around town asking everyone if they have any soda pop bottles they would like to get rid of. There is a deposit you get back for every bottle. You don't even have to wash the bottles first. A lot of people don't want to mess with taking those bottles back so they are more than happy to give them to us.

Sandy comes along to protect us. When we reach Candy's General Store, Katie and I take turns going into the store with Billie. He takes forever picking out a comic book. Sandy is real glad one of us stays out with her. She gets lonesome outside by herself. She just wags her tail as people go in and out of that store hoping someone will stop to pet her.

We all get a vanilla ice cream cone to eat on the way home. I always save a little bit of the ice cream in the bottom of my cone for Sandy to lick. She sure does enjoy those cones as much as we do. Mama tells us not to give her too much; milk can make dogs sick.

• • •

When we arrive back home, Frank is already there. We just know there will be a lot of questions. We hope our answers don't make him mad.

"Where is your Mama and why isn't supper ready?"

"Mama went fishing with Aunt May after work. Without money from Sammy, Mama doesn't have as much money to spend on groceries. She has to save every penny she can. That includes feeding us fish as much as she can!" Katie tells him.

"Where did she go fishing?"

"Mama didn't tell us where they went, Frank."

"How come you kids didn't make anything for supper?"

"Mama said we could make anything we wanted for supper and we aren't hungry yet."

Frank looks angrier than we have ever seen him. "Don't get smart with me, Katie. You find something to cook. I'm hungry. I'm not going to wait all night till your Mama gets home! Do you hear me?"

Katie and I look at each other worried... Frank's face is real red. I doubt it is from being out in the sun. He still has his white shirt and tie on.

"What do you think we should cook, Katie?"

"I don't know. I don't know how to cook like Mama. You look in the pantry. I'll look in the refrigerator. Maybe we can find something!" Katie directs me.

"I found some macaroni shells. What does Mama use them for, Katie?"

"She makes goulash with macaroni shells. Do we have any tomato soup? I know we have Mama's fresh canned whole tomatoes in a jar in the pantry," Katie says to herself more than me.

Katie and I find two cans of tomato soup. "Do we need anything else?"

"Look for an onion. I'll see if we have any hamburger in the refrigerator. While you're at it, see if we have any bread left in the bread box?"

"There's half a loaf left from lunch."

"Mama has hamburger in the refrigerator. I guess we can try to make goulash for supper. You open the cans of tomato soup and the jar of tomatoes. Squish the tomatoes in a bowl for me. And, Missy, make sure you wash your hands good first!"

"Billie, take Sandy outside, and read your new comic book. We don't want Sandy making Frank any madder than he already is!"

"Oh boy, come on, Sandy. I'll read you my new comic book."

"Missy, set the table. Don't forget to set a place for Frank. I'll tell Frank and Billie when supper is ready."

Katie's goulash is pretty good. The pasta is a tiny bit overdone, but it still has the same flavor as Mama's. We always like our goulash best reheated anyway. No one says a word while we eat supper. I think we are afraid we might make Frank mad. Billie ties Sandy up to the clothesline. We don't need her begging at the kitchen table tonight with Mama not here to protect her.

"Well, Katie, your goulash is almost as good as your Mama's. Maybe I don't need her around anymore with you here to cook my meals and clean. What else can you do well, Katie?" Katie turns and walks to the sink. She drops her glass of milk, and it spills all over the kitchen floor. I can see tears running down her cheek. She keeps her back to Frank.

Frank glares at us. "I'll leave you kids to clean up this mess you made before Dot gets home. We wouldn't want her to get the idea I made you make my supper, now would we?"

"What's Mama going to say about us making goulash without her home, Katie? You know how mad she got at Sammy for taking her eggs."

"I don't know. If we tell her Frank made us make him supper we will just cause an argument between them. Why don't you two tell Mama she said we could make anything we wanted, and we were hungry for her goulash!"

"That's a good idea, Katie. Frank looks real mad already!"

"I agree. I hope Mama gets home soon, for all our sakes!" Katie says trembling.

Mama arrives home at bedtime. Frank is waiting in the living room for her. He has been in the red velvet overstuffed chair all night, not doing anything but sitting there in the dark drinking beer. He even leaves the empty bottles on the floor by the chair.

We greet Mama at the garage door. We don't want her to go in the living room unprepared for Frank.

Katie whispers. "Frank's in the living room in the dark passed out. He hasn't been in a good mood all night. He asked a lot of questions about you fishing with Aunt May."

"Mama, Katie made us goulash for supper," Billie tells her.

"Katie, why did you make such a big meal for supper?"

"Ah—we were hungry for your goulash, Mama."

"Frank was hungry and told Katie to make him supper right now, Mama!" Billie tells her, forgetting it was supposed to be a secret.

"Is that true, Katie?"

"Yes, Mama, but it was okay. Missy and I had fun cooking supper together."

Mama throws her car keys on the table. "You kids don't have to do anything Frank tells you to!"

"Billie, what did I tell you? You can never keep a secret. No wonder Mama doesn't want to take you fishing with her!" Katie scolds him.

Mama hands Katie a brown package which we assume contains catfish. She tells her to put the package in the freezer. Then she stomps off to the living room to confront Frank.

I whisper to Katie, "Aren't you glad the catfish went into the freezer?"

"Sure am!"

Mama wakes Frank. "Don't you ever tell my girls to make you supper again. You can eat all your meals out from now on.

I'm not spending another dime on groceries for you. And it's none of your damn business where I am. We are through. There is no more us. Now find a place to live and leave us alone!"

"I see you're still wearing the pearl ring I gave you. You can just take it off your finger. If we are through, you aren't keeping a damn thing I bought you. I'll see to it!" He gives Mama an evil grin.

"You aren't taking this ring or anything else that belongs to me. You didn't pay any rent or buy groceries, you owe me!"

"We'll see about that. There is more than one way to remove the ring from your finger!" Frank says, as he stomps off to the study.

It isn't long before we hear Frank snoring. We walk into the kitchen where it is quiet. Mama decides to heat up some of Katie's special goulash.

"Girls, this goulash is as good as mine. I better start letting you do more of the cooking!"

"I added some sugar to the goulash just like you do, Mama."

Mama winks at Katie. "I didn't know you knew my secret ingredient."

Katie's smile shows how proud she is of herself. She has made Mama happy with her cooking, and she helped stop a fight between her and Frank.

Mama turns the radio on in the kitchen and sings country western songs until two. She goes to bed taking Sandy with her instead of Frank. We know Mama is in good hands with Sandy in her room. We will all get some sleep.

Chapter Seventeen

Frank leaves for work earlier than usual. Mama has to work at Dixon Inn and Victory Bar & Grill today. We will be home by ourselves all day and most of the night. We sure hope Frank stays away. *At least we have left-over goulash for supper.*

Mama has a surprise visitor just before she leaves for work. We kids are curious as an old cat. We know Mama will be mad if she knows we listen at the window upstairs, but us being kids we can't resist.

"Dody Canfield?"

"That's me, the last I looked. How can I help you?"

"I don't think you remember me, but we met a couple of years ago at Castle Rock Restaurant and Bar. I'm Frank Billing's wife, Rhonda Billings. I mean his ex-wife. Do you have a minute so we can talk about Frank?"

We kids didn't even know old Frank had been married before. This woman is gorgeous, and young. She has to be in her early thirties. *Why did Mama and Frank keep his marriage a secret? What could be so important that his ex-wife has come to see Mama? We don't usually have strangers call on us. Does Frank have kids?*

We tiptoed to the register in the floor. Mama greets Frank's ex-wife through the screen door in the kitchen.

"It's good to see you again, Rhonda."

"Would it be all right if I come in?"

Mama opens the door for her visitor. "I'm sorry, come on in. Would you like a cup of coffee?"

"That would be nice. Is Frank here?"

"No. Are you here because you want Frank back? If you are, you can have that sorry S.O.B!"

"That's not why I'm here. I'm concerned for your safety. Do you have any children? If you do, then you better be concerned about their safety, too!"

"Rhonda, I don't know why you're here after all this time, but I can assure you we're through. As you probably already know, that man doesn't help contribute any money toward household expenses. At least he's not ever given me a dime. And he seems to sleep with whatever woman will have him!"

Rhonda stares at Mama's hands. "Did Frank give you the pearl ring you are wearing?"

"Yes. Why?"

"Because it used to be my ring before he took it and gave it to you. He gave that ring to me and told me the pearl on the gold band is as pure as our love for one another."

"That is exactly what Frank told me when he gave me this ring; after he slept with Caroline. How could he give me someone else's ring? Do you want the ring back? Is that why you're here?"

"To answer your question, no. I didn't know until now he gave you my ring. It doesn't mean a thing to me anymore. Did Frank ever buy you new clothes every time you got into a fight? He was always showering me with presents after we argued!"

"Yes, sometimes, but what does that have to do with you coming to my home after all this time?"

"Do you have any children?" she asks again.

"Yes, I have three. Why do you want to know?"

"I'm worried about your children's safety and yours!" She begins pacing in the kitchen.

"Has Frank ever been violent when he's been drinking? He always got violent with me!"

"We've had our share of fights, Rhonda, but so do a lot of couples."

"I'm not talking about some little lover's quarrel. Frank frightens me! I think he is capable of killing someone!"

Billie whispers. "Katie, is that woman talking about our Frank?"

"Shh...we can't hear!"

Mama drops her cup of coffee on the floor; shattering it. She begins trembling.

Rhonda asks her if she is all right. She tells her she is fine;

just a little shocked. She gets a broom and cleans up the broken cup before she sits back down with Rhonda.

"What makes you think Frank is capable of killing someone?"

"Is it okay if I call you, Dot?"

"That's what everyone calls me!"

"I suppose I should start at the beginning. We were married for only a year when everything started going wrong. Every time I would even look or talk to another man, Frank got jealous. Sometimes he didn't even have to be drinking to start an argument. I couldn't even go to the grocery store without him. He thinks every woman messes around. Not to say that he hasn't done his share of flirting and staying out all night. He always brought me presents to make up. I have a whole closet full of new clothes he purchased for me."

"A lot of men purchase gifts for their girlfriends or wives to make up. I see it all the time where I work. What makes Frank doing it any different?"

"We had this female black lab, Lizzy, who had five puppies. They were the cutest little puppies that I ever did see. One day, I heard Lizzy barking frantically out in our garage. When I went to see what all the barking was about, I saw Frank holding a large dog food bag in his hands, dripping with blood. There on the floor lay five puppy heads with no bodies. Blood was everywhere!"

"Frank had—"

"Katie, that woman said her dog ate her puppies like

Calico."

She placed her hand gently over Billie's mouth. "I need you to be quiet for a while. I can't hear what they're saying!"

"My dog, Lizzy was never the same. I had to get rid of her. Frank said he had to—"

"Doesn't old Frank like dogs?"

Katie whispers. "Billie, do I have to put tape over your mouth. Mama might hear us. You have to be quiet!"

Mama's face turns as white as old Frank's shirts.

"Dot, are you okay? Do you need a drink of water or anything?"

Mama just sits in her chair for a few minutes not saying a word. She looks stunned.

"Are you okay?" Rhonda asks again.

"I'm ...okay just a little shocked and sad. Rhonda, we had a cat, Calico, whom I loved dearly. She had a litter of kittens. She brought us one of the kitten's heads; without the kitten's body. When we went to the barn to check on the rest of her kittens there were no bodies, just the heads. We thought Calico had eaten her kittens' bodies. I took her out in the country and dumped her off by a farm. I feel so bad!"

"Katie, why are they talking about Calico?"

"Shh...for the last time, you have to be quiet!"

"You know, Dot, Frank is dangerous! That isn't the worst part; there's more."

"How could there be more? Isn't this bad enough?"

"Frank and I got a divorce about a year ago. It was a bitter and difficult divorce." She wipes away tears. "He asked for everything; including the pearl ring. He told me he wasn't going to let me have anything he ever bought or gave me and he meant it. But the judge didn't see it like Frank did. I got to keep everything. He sent me nasty letters every week. He called me and threatened to kill me if he caught me with another man. I saw him peeking in my windows at night. It was a long time before I slept through the night!"

"The other day when we had a fight, Frank did sleep on a hammock outside my bedroom window!"

"Dot, that's not all. I met this man, his name was Henry McDougall. He was forty-two and owned a hardware store in Dixon. The only thing he really liked to do for recreation without me was fish. I don't like to fish, but I didn't mind going out in his boat with him. He kept his boat at a dock in Grand Detour. He was the best thing that ever happened to me. He was kind, gentle, and not a bit jealous like Frank. We were to be married next year. We were even going to start a family!"

"The name Henry McDougall sounds familiar. I know I've heard the name somewhere before," Mama tells Rhonda.

"The name probably sounds familiar because Henry drowned close to your house. He had gone fishing and never returned. He was missing three days before some kids found his body. They ruled his death suspicious. His death is still being investigated!"

"What are the police investigating Henry's death for,

Rhonda? I need to know!"

"They think Henry was confronted by someone. There seemed to have been a struggle. They found Henry's tackle box open and the tackle was scattered all over the bottom of his boat. One of his fishing poles had been broken. If it had been someone planning to steal those items, they wouldn't have broken the poles they would have taken them. They found Henry's blood on one of the oars. The contusion on the right side of Henry's head looked like it might have come from being struck with that oar. His death wasn't an accident. He couldn't have fallen on that oar!"

"What are you trying to tell me?"

"I think Frank—"

"Katie, Missy and I found a man dead while fishing! Do you think the woman Mama is talking to knew him?"

"Billie, be quiet or I'm going to send you to your room!"

"I know Frank has a temper, but I'm not sure he would go that far!"

"You said you have children. Think about them. You need to be careful. Frank is dangerous. You or your kids could be next. I didn't know Frank was living with you until the other day when he let it slip. I felt it was my duty to find where you live and warn you!"

Mama is quiet for a few minutes. I've never known her to be without words. She takes a puff on her cigarette and looks into Frank's ex-wife's eyes. "This is too much for me to take all in. I'll need a while to digest this information!"

"Do you know where Frank has been staying lately?"

"No. I told him to move out a couple of nights ago. He said he stayed with Sam DelRosa."

"He came to my house drunk. I didn't want to let him in, but he still had a key. He tried to—"

Katie covers Billie's ears.

"He told me to remember what he said; he said that there would be hell to pay if he ever saw me with another man in his house. Then he took the pearl ring you are wearing off my finger. He said I was lucky he didn't cut my finger off to get the ring! Then he passed out on my couch next to the phone."

"What color of lipstick do you wear, Rhonda?"

"Shimmering Pink, why?"

"I found pink lipstick on Frank's shirt when I did his laundry. But, Rhonda that still doesn't mean Frank killed Henry!"

Frank's ex-wife wipes away tears. "Just think about what I've told you. I don't want Frank to kill anyone else!"

Rhonda leaves Mama sitting in her chair and lets herself out. She doesn't move for quite some time. She just sits quietly; turning the pearl ring on her finger.

"Katie, why does that woman think Frank killed someone?" Billie asks.

She turns in my direction. "I don't know. You know how you exaggerate when you tell Mama stories. I think the woman was exaggerating about old Frank!"

Charlie comes over and takes us all for a ride in his Chevy.

Katie hasn't seen much of him lately. His family always takes their summer vacations in Florida. They have a lot of family that live there.

Sandy seems to have missed Charlie, too. She just keeps licking his face and sniffing his head. Her little tail is wagging almost off her body. He must have missed her. He asks Sandy, "You want to go for a ride, girl?"

Sandy wags her little tail as she licks Charlie's hand.

Charlie takes us all to Candy's General Store to get ice cream cones. We eat them on the picnic table behind the store. I share mine with Sandy. Katie and Charlie missed each other so much they just keep holding hands and looking at each other smiling. *I'm not ever going to like boys like that!*

Charlie is really nice to me and Billie today. He isn't even pulling any pranks on us.

It is sure nice to get away from our house for a little while. We don't even have to worry about old Frank. Sandy doesn't have to worry about him either.

After we eat our ice cream, we head back home and play Monopoly with Charlie. I usually don't like Monopoly, but today playing the game makes me feel safe. It takes a long time to get a winner, and that means Charlie is at our house to protect us from Frank.

Charlie even stays for supper. We heat up the left-over goulash. Katie opens up a jar of Mama's canned green beans and a jar of her applesauce. They even make a can of biscuits in our oven. He tells her that her cooking is just as good as his

Mama's. This makes Katie feel so happy she just gave him a kiss right in front of Billie and me. I almost feel like Mama is home cooking for one of our uncles.

I don't even have to help wash dishes. Charlie volunteers to help Katie. They stay in the kitchen talking and singing to the radio having a good ole time. I don't think Katie ever had so much fun doing dishes before.

One time, Frank told Charlie he knew what was going on between him and Katie. Charlie told Frank there was nothing going on between them except for an occasional kiss. He has more respect for Katie than that. Frank just winked at him and said, "I bet!" Charlie told Katie what Frank said to him. He told her to watch out for Frank; something with him doesn't seem right. Katie told me what both of them said. And I think Charlie is right!

Charlie leaves around ten. He doesn't want Frank mad at him for staying so late. He frightens him, too!

When Mama comes home around two in the morning, she isn't herself. She asks if Frank is home yet. We tell her, no. We haven't seen him all day or night. She tells us she is tired and going to bed. Then she looks at Billie, and tells him to sleep with Sandy tonight. She needs her bed all to herself.

Chapter Eighteen

The sun is shining and there is a breeze coming in our kitchen window. Mama makes us all French toast and pork sausage patties for breakfast. She even heats up our pure maple syrup. We drink orange juice while Mama sips on her black coffee. She sits at the kitchen table until her ash tray is full of cigarette butts. There isn't any country western music playing in our kitchen on her radio today. She isn't singing like usual. Sandy isn't howling to the music. Mama just sits in her kitchen chair, quiet. Not even answering us if we ask her questions.

After breakfast, Mama tells us to gather up all our throw rugs so they can be washed. First we hang them out on the clothesline and beat them with our broom to get some of the dirt out. Then she washes them in our old wringer washer. It is a great day to hang out rugs on our clothesline with the warmth of the sun and gentle breeze. Katie and I are just glad we aren't hanging out any uncle's boxer shorts. With no clothes being washed, we won't even have ironing.

Mama looks tired. I don't think she got much sleep. Her eyes are swollen and blood shot. Maybe she is worried about Aunt May. She has been meeting Aunt May a lot lately by herself. We haven't even got to go over to Aunt May's to play with Bobby and Rita lately. There sure must be something important going on. We usually get to see our cousins at least once a week.

After laundry, Mama takes a long bath, curls her hair with bobby pins, and paints her nails. She is still really quiet.

"Kids, Aunt May wants to talk to me again today. I'm going to fry us all up some chicken and make some potato salad. While I'm finishing getting ready, you can pack a picnic basket for me and Aunt May. Save yourself some of the food for supper. You can eat your chicken cold later. Don't wait up for me tonight. Aunt May and I might even fish until the sun comes up. If Frank happens to come back, just tell him they called me into work tonight and I'll be late."

"Okay Mama, but we haven't gotten to see Bobby or Rita for a while. Next time you and Aunt May need to talk, can we come with?" Katie asks.

"We'll see. Maybe Aunt May won't need to talk to me after tonight. Let's hope so anyway. Make sure you go to bed early. Don't let anyone come over while I'm gone!"

"I promise we'll be good while you're gone, Mama!" Katie tells her.

"I love you and I'll see you in the morning. You kids listen to Katie now and do what she tells you!"

"We will," we both say, not happy with the idea Katie is babysitting us again.

It was more fun at the river when Katie went to the neighbor boy's trailer and listened to music. At least there she left us alone, and we didn't have anyone bossing us around. And we had someone to play with. Today is going to be very boring with nothing to do. Katie will probably call Charlie on the phone and giggle the whole time. Billie will go out and play with his army men. I guess I will have to sneak into the study and find my Hardy Boys, *The House on the Cliff,* book to read. Old Frank told us we couldn't go into the study anymore with his stuff being in there. *My books are in there and they belong to me not him.*

The study is a disaster. Frank's stuff is all over the floor. His clothes are thrown on his cot and my book shelf is a mess. I sure hope he moves out soon before he ruins everything in the study. Mama worked too hard for Frank not to take better care of it.

When I reach for my book, something rolls out from behind it. It looks like Daddy's wedding ring. I look inside the ring to be sure it isn't Frank's. Mama said Uncle Riley didn't find it at Daddy's accident site. I looked inside the ring to see if the inscription Mama had the jeweler engrave was on the inside. Sure enough. The writing says, "Love always, Dot."

Maybe Uncle Riley found the ring and Mama dropped it when she was decorating. *I'll have to remember to ask her tomorrow.*

We eat supper around six. Mama's fried chicken is just as good cold as it is hot. It is sure nice of her to fix us some food for supper before she went fishing with Aunt May. Old Frank isn't home to bother us so we really are enjoying our food for a change.

Billie eats three pieces of chicken all by himself. I don't know where such a skinny little boy puts all that food. I suspect some of the food went under the table to Sandy. She sure is sticking to Billie's side. She knows better than to beg from me. I want to eat all my chicken myself. And Katie won't give any animals any of her food. Fried chicken is one of the only meats she likes to eat.

"Missy, after dishes are done, do you want to go outside and pretend we are walking on a tight rope at the circus?" Billie asks.

"Sure, but we can't put the rope up too high. I don't want to break my leg or get injured again while Mama is gone. She will really be mad at us if she has to have someone go and find her before she is finished fishing. And Aunt May might be mad if she doesn't get to finish talking to Mama. After all, Mama said this might be the last time they have to meet in private."

Billie and I tie a rope between two trees. We both have to pull the rope as tight as we can so we can walk across it. We saw it done at a circus once. There was even a lady at the circus that had a beard just like a man's.

"Missy, are you going to wear shoes or go barefoot?"

"I'm going barefoot, silly. You know I can't even take one step with my shoes on!"

"I'm going to go barefoot, too!"

Billie always copies me.

We get two of Mama's ladders to put up next to each end of where the rope is tied to the trees. Then we get our pillows from our bedrooms, a couple of old quilts and place them underneath the rope. This is our net. Maybe the pillows will help keep us from breaking our necks. Once we master this height, Billie and I can raise our rope up higher. Maybe we can even reach the top of the tree.

"I want to go first!" Billie exclaims excited.

"Okay, but you better take it slow." Billie starts walking across the rope and begins giggling. "You're not going to cross this rope laughing, Billie!"

Billie giggles more than most girls I know. Maybe he laughs to hide how sad he really is without Mama being home much. His eyes always look sad, but he still giggles.

"Look, I'm almost across!" Billie says, laughing as he falls off the rope.

"See, I told you to stop giggling. You might have made it all the way across on your first try."

"You probably won't make it as far as I did without giggling!"

"I'm going to make it across on my first try. You just watch and see. I don't have Bobby here to help you shake my rope!"

Sandy starts barking at me. Even she doesn't think I will make it across. I will show them both I can make it on the first try. I climb up the ladder, put one foot on the rope, and grab a tree branch with my right hand. The rope feels sturdy enough. I let go of the branch and take one step, hanging onto the rope with my toes. Then I take another step, still keeping my balance.

"Missy, likes boys…Missy, likes boys….." Billie taunts me.

Even Sandy starts barking, agreeing with Billie.

"I do not like boys and you know it, Billie Canfield. Take that back!"

Just as I start to take another step, Sandy begins growling. I turn to look. Frank is headed straight for Billie and me. I lose my balance and over I go, landing on the pillows we placed under the rope.

"Does your Mama know you have your pillows and blankets outside on this dirty, dusty ground?"

"No, but I don't think she will care," I remark.

"Don't get smart with me, Missy Canfield! Where is your mother? Her car's not in the garage."

"I don't know. You'll have to ask Katie."

"Where is Katie?"

"I think she's inside painting her nails."

Sandy growls louder the closer Frank gets to Billie and me. She even shows him her pretty white teeth.

"You kids better get hold of your mangy mutt." Frank says, showing his teeth too as he turns to walk toward the house.

"Come on, Billie. Get your stuff. We better go inside and help Katie with Frank. He looks a bit strange. And, Billie, don't say a word about Mama fishing. You might make Frank crazier than he already is."

"I promise, Missy. I won't say a word this time. I don't want to get Mama into trouble, but what about Sandy?"

Billie wraps his arms around his dog and gives her a big hug. "We don't want him to kick you again, girl. Do we, Sandy?"

As we approach the house, we hear Frank yelling at Katie. He wants to know where his supper is and why we didn't save him any fried chicken. "Your Mama knows fried chicken is my favorite, and you kids should know it by now, too!"

Katie tries telling him she didn't know he was coming back home or she would have saved him some, but he won't listen.

"Where is Dot, Katie? She isn't supposed to work tonight. It is her night off. Why isn't she home?" He screams at her as he slams the refrigerator door.

We see Katie trembling. "Mama got called into work. Someone called in sick and they are short on help. She told us not to wait up for her. She will be working late tonight. You know she needs all the money she can get, Frank!"

I wanted to tell him that if he paid Mama rent, she wouldn't be so broke.

"Are you sure that's where she really is, Katie? You kids better not be covering up for her!"

"Billie, is Katie telling the truth?"

"I think so. Mama told me she was going to work and that I'd better listen to what Katie says. She also told me not to stay up late!"

"You better be telling me the truth, Billie!"

"I am, I promise!" Billie says.

I think this is the first time Billie ever told a lie without giggling. Mama will be proud of him when she finds out how he tried protecting her. Later, Billie tells us he crossed his fingers behind his back. *I'll have to make sure his hands aren't behind his back when I ask him if he is lying or not from now on.*

We can hear Frank mumbling about whether or not Mama is actually at work as he slams the door to the garage.

Katie gives Billie a kiss on the cheek. "I'm proud of you for not telling Frank where Mama really is!"

"He sure is mad. Do you think he's going to go to Victory Bar & Grill and look for Mama?" I ask.

"I don't know, but I hope not. He's already mad enough. Maybe he'll go stay with Sammy and not come back home tonight."

"I hope so. Mama already looks worried and she said Frank frightens her, too." I'm worried about what old Frank might do to her if he finds out she isn't really at work. I know one thing, we best keep Sandy in Billie's room tonight or Frank might take his anger out on her.

Frank doesn't come home all night. For that matter, neither does Mama, which is unusual for her. We sure hope Frank didn't find her fishing and make good on his threats. I'll have to wait until another day to ask her about Daddy's ring.

Chapter Nineteen

When we wake up in the morning, Mama isn't in her bed. Her bed is still made, there are no wrinkles in her covers, and she is nowhere in the house. She hasn't left us any notes, and she hasn't even called.

Frank hasn't been home all night either. There are no new cigarette butts in the ash tray in the study, and the toilet lid in the bathroom is still down. We sure hope he didn't find Mama and start a fight. Maybe they are both in jail.

We try calling Aunt May, but no one answers the phone at her house. Maybe Mama and Aunt May are catching so many fish they don't want to stop fishing. But, Mama is supposed to work at the Dixon Inn today. She never misses work; she needs the money too much. Maybe they gave her the day off and she forgot to tell us.

Sometimes Mama has car trouble. Maybe her car broke down and she had to walk home. I sure hope nothing happened to her and she isn't in the hospital. The memory of

Daddy's death is still fresh in my mind.

It was a full moon out last night. Maybe some bats flew down and took Mama and Aunt May off to some far away cave. I sure wish we knew if Mama is with Aunt May and they are all right. Dracula might have them by now. Maybe they are even his brides like in the movies. I wouldn't want anyone to have to put a stake through my Mama's heart.

With Mama not being home, Katie decides she is our boss. She bosses Billie and me the first thing. *Sometimes I think Katie thinks she is our mother.*

"You kids go make your beds. I'll make us some breakfast. Do you want oatmeal or cream of wheat and toast?"

I love cream of wheat, but you can't ever get that stuff off your bowls if you let your dishes set for a while.

"I want oatmeal, how about you, Billie?" I suggest to him, thinking about doing the dishes later, knowing he copies me.

"I want oatmeal, too. Can we have some of Mama's plum jelly on our toast?" Billie asks. "Where is Mama, Katie? Did she have to go to work early?"

"I don't know. I think she must still be fishing. She probably lost track of time if those fish are biting good."

"Yeah, I sure wish I was fishing with her. She's probably caught Old Moe by now." Billie slumps down into his kitchen chair pouting. "I thought I caught Old Moe, but he turned out to be some dead man!"

We eat our breakfast in silence. Everyone is wondering

where Mama really is. I sure hope she comes home soon. Frank looked crazy when he left our house last night.

Katie worries about Mama all morning. After dishes, she waits by the phone. She tries calling Aunt May several times, but there is still no answer.

She tries calling Grandma Irene, but Roy says she is out working in her garden and he will have her call later. Work is always more important to him than the family, except Caroline.

Katie even tries calling the Dixon Inn, but their line is busy. She thinks about calling Uncle Riley, but if Mama is just fishing and he sends his deputies to look for her, Mama will ground her for life. Besides, if Frank and Mama are fighting they might just take us kids away from her and send us to the orphanage.

"Maybe we should try calling Sammy. He might know where Frank is at least," I say.

"I don't want that man to know Mama isn't home. Have you forgotten about what he tried to do to us?"

"No, I guess that was a bad idea!"

"It sure was! I forgive you. I know you are only trying to help."

Billie's stomach is growling. "Do you think Mama will be home for supper tonight, Katie?"

Katie tries dialing Aunt May again, but with no luck. "We'll just have to wait and see."

I have some money saved from babysitting. Do you guys

want to take a walk along the river with Sandy and me? Then we can go to Candy's General Store for ice cream."

Billie and I just look at each other. Neither of us want anything to do with walking along the river by the dock even if it is to see if Mama is fishing there. "Mama will probably be home soon. I'd rather wait for her, wouldn't you, Billie?"

"Yeah, I'd rather wait here. I don't want to take a walk by the river today either."

"Okay, but if you guys change your mind and want to go for ice cream, let me know. I think I'll try calling the restaurant again and see if they know where Mama might be."

Finally, Katie gets through to Dixon Inn. One of the waitresses answers the phone and tells Katie that Mama took a couple of days off for vacation. She never told any of us we were going on vacation. Usually, we spend our vacation at Castle Rock if she has time off from work. Mama told us she needs to work all she can to pay the bills.

Katie washes the counter for the third time. "Mama better bring home a lot of fish for making us do all this worrying."

Mama doesn't arrive home for lunch. She doesn't even arrive home by supper. She has never stayed away for a whole night and day before. I don't think she even took enough bait to fish this long. Of course, she can go into the river and catch some crawdads or minnows, but Mama usually prefers to use chicken liver to catch catfish. Sometimes she uses night crawlers, but not as much during the day.

"I'm hungry. What are we going to have for supper,

Katie?" Billie asks.

"I don't know, how about tomato soup and tuna sandwiches?"

"Boy, if Mama was home we would be eating her fried catfish instead of tuna!"

"Tuna will have to do for tonight. We can't wait for Mama forever and we don't have anything else thawed out!"

"Billie, why don't you open the cans of tuna and Missy can show you how to make it while I make our soup."

Billie starts to open the cans of tuna when Katie suddenly starts yelling at him. "Billie, your hands are filthy! Go wash your hands before you touch anything else. You too, Missy. Now!"

Billie heads to the bathroom crying. "You didn't have to yell at me. I'm just a little kid. I sure wish Mama was home."

"Come here, Billie. I'm sorry. I didn't mean to yell at you. I'm just worried about Mama. Can I give you a hug? Do you forgive me?"

"I guess so. Do I still get to make the tuna?"

"Sure, but wash your hands first."

Just as Billie returns from the bathroom, the kitchen door opens. At first, we think it is Mama, but Sandy knows different. She growls and shows her teeth. It is old Frank, and he looks meaner than an old grizzly bear.

"Have you kids seen or heard from your Mama? She wasn't at work last night and she wasn't at work this morning. If you know where she is, you best tell me now before I do something you will regret. I told you kids to keep your dog away from me!"

"Billie, go tie Sandy to the clothesline and stay outside with her until I call you for supper."

"Okay, I'm going. Come on, Sandy, before you get into trouble with Frank!" Sandy follows Billie out into the back yard with her tail wagging the whole way. She won't be wagging her tail for long when she finds out Billie is going to tie her up.

"Now you better tell me where Dot is. I don't want to hear any more lies from either of you!"

Katie leans on the counter. Her tan face pales. "We don't know where Mama is! She told us she was going fishing with Aunt May and that Aunt May wanted to talk to her about something private!"

"Is that true, Missy?"

"That's all I know. I haven't seen Mama since yesterday. I'm worried!"

"Your Mama better be with your Aunt May or the next time I see her I will kill her and whoever she is with. Do you hear me? You better tell her I'm looking for her if you know where she's at. I'm going to go to May's and see if she's there or if she knows where Dot is. If she's not there, I'm coming back here and I'm going to kill all you brats and that mangy dog of yours!" Frank slams the screen door so hard he breaks the spring.

"Do you think Frank will kill us and Mama, too?" I ask. I

begin crying, frightened of what Frank might do. His ex-wife said she thought he already killed the man Billie and I fished out of the river!

"I don't know, Missy. Frank smells like a brewery. Maybe he's just drunk and doesn't know what he's saying. If we're lucky, maybe he'll drink some more beer and pass out somewhere. We better not take any chances. We better eat our supper quick and hide somewhere just in case he does come back. Missy, tell Billie to leave Sandy tied up. We don't want her to get in Frank's way if he does return!"

Walking to go get Billie, I tell Katie, "I sure wish Mama hadn't gone fishing!"

"I wish she hadn't gone, too." Katie replies.

Chapter Twenty

Katie tries calling Aunt May but the line is busy. Then she tries calling Grandma Irene again. There is no answer at her house.

"Grandma's usually home. Why do you think she doesn't answer, Katie?" I ask.

"You know Roy. He makes Grandma work from sunup to sundown. He never lets her rest. Not even on Sunday!"

"What about Aunt May?" Billie asks, not having heard any of the other conversations.

"Aunt May's phone is busy. Maybe they took their phone off the hook so they don't have to talk to Frank," Katie suggests, trying not to alarm him.

"I'm really scared! Do you think Frank will come back and get us?"

"I'm afraid too, Billie. I think Frank's really dangerous!"

"Why don't we try calling Charlie? Maybe he will protect us," Billie suggests to Katie.

"You know, Billie that is a great idea. I should have thought of it myself. Thanks! I'll call him now; let's cross our fingers he's home."

Katie dials Charlie's number. She lets it ring several times, but still no one answers.

Billie asks, "Now what are we going to do, Katie?"

"We better hurry up and finish our supper before Frank comes back. Then we better clean up this mess. We don't want to make Mama mad, too if she comes home soon."

We finish cleaning up the kitchen and then we take turns going to the bathroom. Katie tells us to pretend we are going on a primitive camping trip out in the woods without Mama, no bathrooms, no water, no tents. We will have to take a thermos of water and something already prepared in a can to eat.

"You kids change your clothes and put something dark on. You can wear brown, dark blue or black. Just don't wear anything with light colors. It will make it easier for Frank to find us in the dark."

"Why don't we just call Uncle Riley, Katie?" I ask.

"Remember what the police said the last time Mama and Frank fought!"

Billie is frightened, but I don't think he knows the real danger we are in. And he thinks hiding from old Frank is a new adventure.

"Katie, can we pretend we are fishing and take some cans of sardines in mustard sauce with us to eat?"

"I suppose, but I think it might be fun to pretend we are

bird watching. We will have to all be real quiet and see how many different species we can spot."

"I'd rather pretend we are fishing! I don't want to spot any old dumb birds, and you have to be quiet when you are fishing so you don't scare the fish away."

"How about we take a jar of Mama's pickles with us to eat along with your sardines? Missy, go give Sandy some food and water. Make sure she's tied up real good to the clothesline so she doesn't get loose. Hurry up before Frank gets back. We'll meet you behind the bushes by the back porch."

There are a lot of thick bushes close to our house. Frank won't be able to see us, but we will be able to keep an eye on the house in case Mama or Frank comes back.

"I wish Sandy could be with us. Can't we tie her to one of the bushes close?"

"Now, Billie, that won't work. Her barking will give us away. Frank will know exactly where we are!"

"Katie, do you think Mama's ever going to come home again?"

"I hope so, Billie. I sure miss her. I'm even tired of giving you kids' orders." She laughs.

"I hope we never have any more uncles. I hate having to sit behind these bushes because we are afraid of what old Frank might do to us if he finds us!"

Katie sighs. "I don't like sitting on this dirty ground either, but we have no choice. I don't want any more whining. I'm doing the best I can!"

We can hear birds singing. Flies are buzzing around us. We watch the ants crawling on the ground and hear crickets rubbing their legs together to sing. We are aware of every noise around us. All we can do is watch for Mama to return home or Frank to come back and kill us. The thought of Frank makes the hair on my arms stand straight up. Soon it will be dark. There are no snakes slithering around on the ground near us now, but how will we watch for them in the dark. The only snake that will probably be dangerous anyway will be old Frank.

We just sit there waiting, watching, and hoping Mama returns home before Frank does. Maybe if we are lucky, he might find another woman to move in with.

"Can we eat our sardines now? I want to pretend we are fishing and caught our supper. You can pretend that you cooked them, Katie."

"Okay, how would you like your fish cooked, with mustard sauce or fried in beer?"

"I'd like mine in mustard sauce, please!"

"If you don't mind, I'll just eat some pickles. Anyone else want a pickle?" Katie asks. "Maybe later, our fish is enough for now," Billie and I say, licking the mustard sauce off of our fingers.

"What are we supposed to do with our garbage?" we ask.

"Just give it to me. I'll throw it at the edge of the bushes to keep the bugs away from us. I'm sure the smell of those sardines will attract flies. It's a good thing that Frank doesn't have a nose like Sandy's. He'd find you two just from the smell!"

"Yeah, we smell almost as good as the river on a hot day, don't we, Missy?"

"I guess we do smell like rotten fish. We can't even wash our hands off or brush our teeth."

It is uncomfortable sitting on the hard ground, with nothing to do but wait. Mama has never been gone this long. It is getting dark and a breeze has picked up. The ground is cooling off and getting damp. It sends shivers through my body.

"I wish we thought to bring some pillows and blankets with us. Can we run in the house and get some blankets, Katie?"

"No! Are you crazy? Frank could come back anytime. You'll just have to sit here and wait for Mama to come home!"

"Do we have any blankets hanging out on the clothesline?"

"I don't think so, Missy. We do have some throw rugs on the line we could lay on. You keep Billie here and I'll sneak over and get the rugs."

Katie crawls to the clothesline. We see Sandy wagging her tail at Katie. Sandy thinks she is going to let her loose to be with us. If Frank comes home now, he surely will suspect we are out in the back yard.

It takes two trips for Katie to get all the rugs. We each have a couple of rugs to sit on and one to wrap around our shoulders. They aren't as soft as blankets, but they will keep the chill off and make the hard ground a bit softer.

"This is just like waiting for a fish to bite. Isn't it, Missy?"

"Sure is! You have to sit and wait quietly for both."

"How many fish have you caught now, Missy?"

"I have only caught one small fish. My fish keep getting away!" I say, thinking about old Frank's big lips and how I wish Mama hadn't reeled him in. And I hope he doesn't end up being Mama's fatal catch!

The moon is full and bright orange. This makes it easier to see each others' face. If we aren't careful, it will make it easier for Frank to see us, too. Bats are flying around at the top of our trees. Katie tells us to keep our hair covered up with the rugs so the bats don't get tangled up in our hair. I am hoping those bats stay away from us and don't turn into vampires and carry us away. *I sure wish Katie hadn't taken us to the outdoor theater to see that Dracula movie. I also wish Mama was here to give us all a big hug and kiss. I want her to protect us from old Frank. She just has to be alive!*

Chapter Twenty-One

Katie tries keeping Billie quiet. We have been sitting out on these rugs for several hours, and he is bored. It is getting harder to quietly entertain him. His patience has run out as well as ours.

"Katie, can I sneak into the house and get some of my army men to play with?"

"No! Frank might come home and find you. Now sit still and be quiet. If you can't do that, then lay on your rug and go to sleep."

A barn owl is checking our yard out for any small critters to eat. The neighbors' dogs are busy letting Sandy know what is going on in the neighborhood.

"Shh…listen. Do you hear something, Missy?" Katie whispers softly.

We hear something or someone walking in our yard, and they are getting close to our hiding spot. Sandy is growling and showing her teeth. A twig snaps not far from us and then another and another. It sounds like something is walking along the edge of the bushes stepping on the brush pile Mama just made trimming. We hear a loud crack. Whatever is breaking the sticks has to be large.

"Missy, Billie, get ready to run if it is Frank." Katie whispers loudly.

Another twig snaps closer this time. Frank must be waiting for just the right moment to attack us; waiting like a lion stalking its prey.

"I'm scared, Katie! Shouldn't we run and hide?" Billie asks frightened.

"Not yet. Not until I yell, run," Katie tries whispering quieter this time but her voice just becomes louder.

Sandy's teeth look bright white in the dark. She has her rope stretched as tight as she can get it trying to get at whatever or whoever is approaching us.

Another twig snaps. Katie grabs Billie and me, and holds on to us as tight as she can, almost choking us to death. Katie lets out an ear piercing scream. We see two eyes glaring at us in the dark. "Look, it's not Frank! It's just a little old raccoon finishing your mustard sauce in those sardine cans!" She fell back down on the ground and started roaring with laughter. Then she puts her head between her knees and begins crying.

"Katie, it is just a little raccoon. You don't need to cry. It will be okay!" Billie tells her, giving her a hug and patting her shoulder.

"It's not that, Billie. It could have been Frank and he could have killed you both. It would be my fault for not protecting you better." Katie gives us both a hug and a kiss on the cheek. "You two sit quiet. I'm going to throw those cans of sardines far away from these bushes. We don't need any more raccoons scaring us. Whatever you do, stay behind these bushes and don't say a word."

It doesn't take Katie long to throw those cans away. We don't need any old raccoons giving our hiding place away. When she comes back, she gives us both another hug. That's the most hugs Katie has ever given me.

"Billie, we have to be real quiet now. If you want, you can go to sleep for a while. We'll wake you up when Mama comes home."

"I think I will. I'm tired," he says yawning.

It isn't long before we see a car slowing down on the road in front of our house. It has to be old Frank. The headlights don't look like Mama's.

"Billie, wake up, Frank's home. We have to be really quiet. If I tell you to run, you run as fast as you can and hide. You too, Missy. Don't wait for me!"

Frank turns on almost every light downstairs. He even turns the back porch lights on. Sandy barks furiously at old Frank.

"If you kids are here, you better get in here and tell me where that tramp of a mother of yours is. Right now!"

The phone starts ringing. *Maybe it's Mama. I wish we could answer it. It is late so it has to be someone we know. Frank stumbles to answer it. We will never be able to get to it now. If it is Mama, she won't know we are out in the yard scared!*

"Hello, who's on this damn phone? If it's you, Dot, you better answer me now! Hello, hello, who is this? Answer me damn it! I know it's you, Dot! Answer me, now!"

Frank screams at the phone like it understands him. No one must have said anything on the other end of the line. *If it is Mama, I hope she knows Frank is drunk and looking for her.*

We watch as Frank takes out his long shiny knife and cuts the cord to our telephone. He picks our phone up and throws it across the living room. *Now we will never know if Mama tried calling us and heard Frank's deranged voice!*

"Why did Frank cut that cord off of our phone, Katie?" Billie asks.

"Shh…Billie, I don't know, but we don't want him to know we are out in the back yard, honey. We have to be real quiet."

"If you kids are here and I find you, I'm going to kill you! Answer me! Where the hell are you brats?" Frank screams, as he goes into the maid's quarters where Mama made her a closet.

He brings all of Mama's clothes out of the room and throws them on her bed. We can see him through Mama's bedroom window. He looks crazier than a rabid raccoon.

He just keeps screaming, "You aren't going to ever wear a damn thing I bought you, Dot. I'm going to see to it. You're not keeping anything I bought for you or belongs to me. I'm tired of women keeping all of my stuff!"

Frank takes Mama's new yellow dress he gave her and starts tearing it up with his bare hands. He just keeps tearing the dress into pieces until there is nothing left.

"If I get a hold of you, Dot, I'm going to cut you into pieces just like this dress. You ought not to have left me!" He screams, as he grabs another dress and starts tearing it, too.

Frank grabs Mama's fur coat that Uncle Riley bought for her. He takes his long knife out of his pocket and starts cutting the fur to pieces like it is paper.

"You're not going to get by with leaving me! Where are you, you rotten bitch? Where are you, you good for nothing kids? You see this coat, you snot nosed brats, that is how I killed those kittens of yours! That is how I'm going to kill all of you and your mangy dog when I find you! That dog of yours won't be the first mutt I've killed!" Frank screams louder and louder with every cut on the coat he makes. It looks like a scene out of one of those movies we saw at the theater. *It has to be a dream. Things like this don't happen to real people. This can't be happening at our house to Mama's things and with her missing.*

Billie cries. "Katie, I'm scared! I've never seen anyone cut stuff up with a knife before! Is Frank really going to kill us with his shiny knife?"

Katie pulls Billie close. "You have to stop crying. Frank might hear you. Then he will find us for sure. We don't know if he's bluffing or has really killed someone before."

"I'll try, but I'm scared!"

Sandy keeps barking and growling at Frank. She tries stretching her rope as far as it will reach. She doesn't like the fact old Frank killed Calico's kittens. Calico was Sandy's best friend. And Mama took Calico for a ride for nothing thinking she ate her kittens' bodies. *"Oh, Calico, I'm so sorry for thinking you could do such a thing to your babies. I didn't know Frank killed them, and to think you tried telling us."*

Frank keeps tearing up dress after dress, blouse after blouse. Mama isn't even going to have any clothes left to wear when she does return home, if she ever does and isn't already dead!

Could Mama have run off frightened of old Frank? Maybe old Frank killed her and doesn't remember. He does seem to be crazy in the head. Oh, Mama, you have to come home soon. Please, God, keep our Mama safe and Katie, Billie, and Sandy, too.

Frank takes all Mama's shoes out of her closet. He keeps throwing them across the bedroom. Then he goes to pick one up and pulls off the heel of that very shoe. When he finishes with the heel, he takes his knife out and cuts the shoe apart. He just keeps cutting up those shoes and removing the heels until there are no shoes left to destroy. How he doesn't get tired from cutting up everything is beyond me. No one in their right mind takes the time to slash every shoe a person owns, especially Mama's. She owns over 30 pairs!

"If you kids are here, when I'm through with Dot's stuff, I'm going to kill you next; especially you, Missy; you know-it-all little brat. You're always causing trouble between your

Mama and me. I think I will kill you first. Katie, you will be the last to die, so you can watch your sister and brother suffer. It will be a pleasure to kill you. I should have let Sam have his way with you. Maybe, I'll have enough fun with you for the both of us before I kill you. You little tramp! You're just like your Mama, kissing on men. She just couldn't stay away from Roger. It's her fault he's dead! It was easier than I anticipated forcing his car off the road and into the river." Frank screams at the top of his lungs. "And your poor daddy; all this time you thought he had an accident. Even Riley couldn't put two and two together. I wanted your Mama and she wasn't going to leave your daddy. I forced his car head on into that telephone pole. I always get what I want! And now if she's with Riley—"

Katie pulls Billie and me closer to her. She puts her arms around us. I think to comfort herself as much as Billie and me. "I'm not going to let that crazed man touch either of you, do you hear me? Just sit here quietly and don't say a word. Maybe he'll pass out drunk or from sheer exhaustion."

"Katie, do you think Frank killed Roger and Daddy?"

"Oh...I'm pretty sure he did it all right! He's not smart enough to make all this up. There's nothing we can do, but wait. Maybe you both better say a little prayer for all of us. That's the only thing that might save us now!"

"Too bad Mama didn't kill old Frank with her rolling pin. He would be buried in our backyard by now instead of him killing all of us!" I whisper.

Frank takes the picture of the nude lady off Mama's bedroom wall he bought her and runs his fingers across the shiny blade. He begins slashing the ladies eyes out, then he takes his knife and jabs it into the ladies neck in the picture, pulling the knife all the way down to the frame.

"Sure wish this was you, Dot. I'd have gotten rid of my pain in my neck for good!" he screams. His screams stop as quickly as they began. He starts laughing hysterically. It is as if we are at the outdoor theater watching some horror movie. *This isn't real. This can't be happening at our house, in our back yard!*

Frank grabs Mama's chenille bedspread next. He tears it into a thousand pieces all by hand. I never knew a bedspread could tear so easily. It takes Grandma Irene forever to tear material into strips for her quilts and rugs. Old Frank makes it look easy.

After Frank tears up Mama's bedspread, he stomps over to her jewelry box. He takes her jewelry out of that box and stuffs it into his pants pockets. Mama isn't even going to have any jewelry left either.

He takes the teddy bear with the beautiful crimson red ribbon around its neck and cuts the bear's head off with his long knife. Then he takes his knife and stabs it where a real heart would be. "When I find you, Dot, I'm going to do the same thing to you I did to this bear!"

We see Frank leave Mama's bedroom. *Maybe he is going to leave. Maybe we will be safe after all.*

Frank doesn't leave. He walks out to the porch and looks

the yard over. We are lucky he doesn't spot us. When he finishes his search, he walks back into the living room straight to the red velvet overstuffed chair he used to kiss Mama in. He just sits in the chair for a few minutes doing nothing but thinking and rubbing the velvet with his fingers. He then wipes his face with a handkerchief and stands back up.

"Dot, how dare you look at another man? Where are you, you tramp? You're never going to sit in this chair with another man again. I'll make sure of it!" He screams at the chair as if Mama is in it.

He takes his knife back out. He stabs the red chair over and over again. After it is full of holes, he takes his long knife and slices it, pulling out stuffing every time the knife connects with the fabric. When he finishes stabbing and cutting the chair, he picks it up and throws it across the room like it is nothing; breaking the legs off. *That chair had been our daddy's. Now we have lost one more memory of him.*

When he is done with the chair, he starts on our couch. He didn't even help purchase the couch or anything. For that matter, he didn't even buy most of Mama's jewelry. The last straw is when he goes out onto the porch and starts cutting up the braided rug Mama's grandma made so lovingly for us using our old clothes. It took her forever to make that rug, not to say we can't replace all of those old clothes which had special memories. *What did Mama's grandma ever do to Frank to deserve this?*

We can tell Frank went into our new study. All the lights

are on in that room. It is on the other side of our house so we can't see through any windows. I sure hope he isn't cutting up all my new books. Frank begins screaming and cussing in our study. We can't make out what he is saying, but he sure sounds mad. Maybe it is better we can't hear him!

Frank comes out of the room with a few of his bags packed. *Maybe he is going to move out after all. If I'm lucky, maybe he didn't destroy my books!*

Frank comes back out onto the porch. We are so close to him I think for sure he hears our hearts pounding.

"If you kids are out in this yard, you can watch me kill your mangy dog before I kill you!" Frank screams, and then his screams turn into laughter.

Frank takes Mama's crazy quilt her grandma made for her; burying his face in it. Then a sound comes out of his mouth that I have never heard before from any human being. It is the scariest sound I have ever heard, including in the movies. It sounds like he's growling while he's screaming. Frank takes that quilt and starts ripping it apart until there is nothing left. Then he just sits down in Mama's white wicker rocker, looking out the porch window, rocking back and forth, not saying a word.

"What do you think old Frank's doing, Katie?" I ask, afraid he spotted us.

"I don't know, but don't you two say another word or move!"

I can feel Katie trembling and her hands are cold as ice.

"Do you think he's going to pass out right there on our front porch in Mama's rocker?"

"Sshh...Missy, don't talk, be real quiet!"

Sandy isn't happy with old Frank sitting on her porch. She just keeps growling at Frank; showing him her pretty teeth.

"If you kids are out there, you better tell that damn dog of yours to shut up before I shut her up for good! It will give me pleasure to get rid of her for good. I can almost feel her warm blood on my hands right now!" Frank screams out the porch window. It's as if he's looking straight at us.

Billie begins crying. "I don't want Frank to kill Sandy. You have to stop him!"

Katie pulls Billie close trying to comfort him. She whispers softly. "Shh...Billie. You have to keep real still or Frank will find us and we will be his next targets. There is nothing I can do right now but try and keep you two safe!"

We hear Frank throwing stuff in the kitchen and slamming the refrigerator door. Frank raises his voice an octave higher. He wants us to know he believes we are still on the property.

"Damn, I'm sure thirsty. Sure could use a good cold beer. Tearing up all this damn stuff sure does make a man work up a thirst. You kids know where your Mama put my beer? It seems as if someone else has drank it all. Your Mama had some other man over here drinking my beer?"

"I'll be back, and when I do, I'll finish what I started. Your Mama's not going to have a damn thing left she ever cared about. I'm not finished with you yet. Don't get too comfortable if you're out there in that yard!"

We see Frank's headlights dim as he drives down the street to the nearest bar. We cross our fingers hoping old Frank doesn't find Mama in the bar.

"Can we go in the house now? I have to go pee!" Billie says.

Katie tries to keep her head turned so we can't see the tears flowing down her cheeks.

"No, Billie, Frank said he's coming back. I think he means every word he is yelling. You can go over to the edge of the bushes and go pee. No one's going to see you. It's dark!"

"What is Mama going to do with all her stuff torn up?"

"I don't know, Missy. Let's just hope Mama is safe and is able to come home again. I'm worried Frank might have found her already. He doesn't seem to be stable. He is crazy and very capable of killing us all!"

"Billie, why don't you try to rest your eyes for a while? We'll wake you up if Frank or Mama return."

Yawning, Billie lays his head on Katie's lap. She rubs his forehead until he falls asleep.

Morning can't come quick enough for me!

Chapter Twenty-Two

Billie falls asleep in Katie's arms. *At least he will have a few minutes of peace before old Frank returns.* If we are lucky, a policeman might stop him for drunk driving. But there usually aren't too many police around our town. Maybe he will get into a fight at the bar. Then they might call the police to come and lock him up for the night.

"Katie, do you think old Frank is really coming back?"

"I'm sure of it! He said he wasn't finished with us yet, and look what he's already done. I bet he'll only be gone long enough to purchase a six pack of beer at the bar. He doesn't look like he's in any mood for conversation!"

"I guess you're right. He doesn't look like he wants to talk to anyone tonight. What's Mama going to wear without any clothes now?"

"That's the least of her worries right now, Missy!"

I stand up. "I'm going to let Sandy loose so she has a fighting chance against old Frank. It's not fair that she's tied up so he can easily grab her!"

"Missy, stop! Come back! If Frank sees her loose, he'll know we are here!" Katie yells.

"Is Frank home, Katie?" Billie asks.

"No, Billie. He isn't home yet."

"Missy, get back here now!"

I run and give Sandy a great big hug. "I'm not going to let old Frank kill you so easily, girl. You're at least going to have a fighting chance, not like Calico's kittens. Poor Calico, she tried telling us, didn't she, girl. You knew all along old Frank was dangerous. That's why you never liked him. We should have listened to you. Oh, Sandy, I love you!"

"Missy, don't let Sandy loose! Listen to me, please?"

Sandy stretches the rope so far the snap sticks. I finally get Sandy's rope loose. "There you go, girl. Now go to where Katie and Billie are!"

Sandy runs straight for the house. She goes inside the open porch door.

"Sandy, come back! Don't go into the house. Frank will find you. Come on, girl. Here, Sandy. I have a biscuit for you," I yell. Sandy isn't falling for my lying about the biscuit. I have used that trick once too often.

Sandy doesn't listen to a word I say. Growling, she keeps her eyes focused on the porch.

I run to Sandy, hoping old Frank doesn't return before I catch her. "Sandy...come here, girl. Let's go outside. Come,

Sandy!"

Sandy runs farther into the house. She only has one thing on her mind, and it is finding old Frank.

"Missy, Frank's coming back. I see his headlights. Run! Get out of the house! Don't worry about Sandy!" Katie yells frantically.

It's too late. I can't go back outside without Frank seeing me and knowing Katie and Billie's hiding place. Sandy is already in the house. Frank suspects we are somewhere on this property. I hope Mama returns before Frank finds us. Maybe he will think Sandy pulled her rope so tight the snap broke.

I hear Frank's car door slam. It won't be long before he is in the house with us.

Sandy begins growling at the kitchen door. I whisper, "Sandy, come here, girl. Come to me!" She just ignores me.

Sandy won't listen to me. I will just have to hope old Frank doesn't suspect someone is in the house with her.

Where am I going to hide? Frank has turned all the lights on in the house except the upstairs. I hate going up those stairs in the dark. A vampire might get me, and there are bats out by the tops of the trees already. It's either the bats or old Frank. At least with the bats, I get to come back to life for a while, well sort of.

I quietly climb the dark stairs that lead up to our bedrooms. The dark usually frightens me, but Frank scares me more than these dark stairs do. If the light is on, he will surely find me.

Knowing a couple of the stairs at the top squeak no matter how hard you try to be quiet, I climb them carefully. I used to try and come down those stairs in the morning to go pee without waking Mama, but they always gave me away. Especially since her bedroom is just below the stairway. I hope Sandy's barking covers up the noise from these squeaky stairs this time.

I'm not going to cry. This dark staircase is a blessing. Maybe old Frank won't be able to find me up here. But, he can turn the light switch on downstairs. He will find me for sure then. I won't even have a chance to escape. There is no place to hide. And it is too far down to jump out my bedroom window.

The light bulb is at the top of the stairs. Maybe I can reach it and take the bulb out. I saw someone do it in the movies once. I try reaching for the light bulb. It is too high up. Every second seems like a minute, and every minute seems like a lifetime. Knowing I don't have much time left, I try reaching for the bulb again; on my tip toes this time using my fingertips. It is taking too long to unscrew this light bulb. I finally manage to get the bulb out. Not having a good grip on the bulb it drops; shattering into a million pieces. I'm sure old Frank has to have heard the bulb break. If I'm lucky, he is busy with Sandy, and her barking is louder than that bulb breaking.

I stand in the dark at the top of the stairs waiting for old Frank to leave again. I hear him yelling at poor Sandy. She is going to be in trouble for sure if she doesn't leave him alone this time.

"Get out of my way, you mangy mutt. Let me finish my

beer. What? Are you in a hurry for me to kill you? Just wait. I'll get around to killing you soon enough you aggravating, ugly dog. God, how I hate animals!"

Old Frank must not have heard me climb the stairs, or he wouldn't be drinking his beer. Maybe he will just drink all six of those beers and pass out like he sometimes does. Then maybe we can sneak out and hide somewhere by the river until we spot Mama's car. Even the river by the dock doesn't scare me as much as old Frank at this moment!

"How did you get loose, Sandy? Did someone let you loose? Come here, girl. Come to your old buddy, Frank. Let me look at your collar!"

Sandy growls at old Frank. She isn't falling for any of his lies.

I hear old Frank trying to catch Sandy. He is chasing her around the living room and kitchen. He will never catch her like that. *I wish I could yell, and tell her to run outside and hide.*

"When I catch you, I'm going to kill you, Sandy. Hold still now and let me see your collar!"

Old Frank must have reached for Sandy as she moved. I hear something big fall to the floor. Maybe old Frank broke his leg or even better; broke his neck!

"Don't you ever try tripping me again! When I get a hold of you, you're dead!"

I guess old Frank didn't get injured from his fall. Poor Sandy! I hear him chasing her around the house again. I hope she's smart enough not to let him get close.

"That's it! I'm tired of chasing you! I am not playing your games anymore! Come on, Sandy. Come to Frank. Get close enough I can throw this old knife into your sorry belly, you fool!"

No, Frank can't do that to Sandy. That's not even fair. I should have left her tied up. She might have been safe. If he kills her, it will be all my fault! Oh, poor Sandy.

I hear Sandy yelp, then a loud thump. I hope old Frank just kicked her again and didn't actually kill her.

Frank screams at Sandy. "Serves you right you damn dog!" Sandy lets out anther yelp, then another. They are the most ear piercing yelps I have ever heard. I try covering my ears, but I still hear her agonizing cries.

Old Frank must be stabbing her like he did the red velvet overstuffed chair of Mama's. I hope she doesn't suffer!

Frank begins pacing the floor. I hope he wears himself out. That might give both Sandy and me a chance to run from him.

"Who let you loose, Sandy? Are those kids in this house? Maybe we better take a look around. It doesn't look like you broke your collar, girl. Are those kids outside? Too bad you can't tell me. Too bad you didn't put up a better fight!" Old Frank screams.

He wants us kids to know he killed Sandy and we are next. If he finds me, I'm going to fight with everything I have to save Billie, Katie and myself. He's not going to kill us so easy!

"I think I'll just sit here and watch old Sandy's blood flow onto the floor while I drink another beer. She sure does have a lot of it. You kids have a lot of blood, too? It's probably yellow by now. Yellow like the cowards you all are!"

It gets quiet for a minute. I peek through the floor register to see what old Frank's up to next. He heads for the refrigerator. As if he needs more beer. Why can't he just pass out? He sits down at the kitchen table and smokes a cigarette. When he finishes, he begins screaming again.

"You kids afraid of little old Frank? What have I ever done to you? It's your Mama I hate. Who's going to be first? Do any of you want to volunteer to be the first one I kill? Or are all of you cowards like your tramp of a Mama? I guess I'll just have to start with whoever is in this house."

I see Frank go toward the bathroom. Maybe I can run out of the house? Frank came out so quick he must have missed that toilet for sure. He heads to the living room and begins pacing again.

"Did Sandy follow you all in here? What were you in the house for? Were you getting a little hungry? If you're upstairs, Missy, I should have killed you when I found you at the cemetery! Your Mama made me go and get you, you little baby! You are too much of a coward to be sitting in the dark alone!

Why doesn't he stop screaming? I can't take him screaming about killing Sandy and Daddy. Please, God, make old Frank leave us alone! Mama, where are you? I begin softly crying.

"Ow! Damn dog, you're still tripping me when you're dead!

"Maybe you are the one in here, Katie. You need to call

your little boyfriend? Too bad I already got rid of the phone. No one is going to help you kids. You're all going to die. It's not like you'll be the first person I have killed with my bare hands. You brats remember that man you found drowned. I killed him, too! He was going to be using everything I bought for my last wife. You probably didn't even know I was married before, did you? Henry McDougall would have lived in the house I bought for me and my ex-wife, Rhonda. No one takes my stuff and lives to tell about it! No one! That includes that tramp of a woman you all call your Mama! And no damn man is going to take my woman! Do you hear me?" He continues screaming.

What am I going to do? I can't let him kill Billie, Katie, or Mama if she's still alive. I don't have any cast-iron skillets up here to hit him with. There aren't any guns or knives upstairs. There is nothing to use for a weapon. Billie does have a wooden baseball bat in the corner of his room. Maybe it will at least knock him out. I have to try something. I can't let him kill anyone else.

I go into Billie's bedroom to look for his bat. *I sure hope he didn't leave it outside the last time he played with it. He is good at not putting his things away.* Making my way around his room in the dark, I trip on some of his army men lying all over his floor. *I hope old Frank didn't hear me downstairs.* I feel around and finally find Billie's bat. I grab hold of it real tight and make my way to the top of the stairs in the dark. My heart is pounding outside my chest. If I knew what a heart attack feels like, it might be what I am feeling right now, in the dark, at the top of these stairs!

"You kids upstairs? You're not really scared of me, are you? I'm just teasing you. You know I haven't really killed anyone. Your mangy dog deserved to die!"

I didn't answer old Frank. I'm not falling for any of his lines. He killed Calico's kittens and Sandy. I'm sure he killed Henry McDougall, and Roger. I sure hope he isn't serious about forcing Daddy into the telephone pole. Mama told us the only thing that helped her get through Daddy's death was that he died instantly, and didn't have time to think about leaving us behind.

"If you kids don't come down here now, I'm coming up there. There is no place to escape. You can jump out one of those windows up there and then you'll die anyway!"

I sure wish I listened to Katie and stayed outside. At least we all had a chance to run if he found us. Now I can't let him find them. It is better if he finds me first and they at least have a chance to escape. Maybe he won't see me in the dark and he will just leave. No matter what, I can't let him find my sister and brother!

I hear old Frank stagger to the stairway. Too bad he didn't drink enough to pass out. Maybe his vision is blurred and I can just run past him. Maybe he is so drunk he will just fall down these stairs.

"I hear you up there. Come down, now!" He screams as he steps on the first stair. If you tell me where your Mama is, I might let Billie live. What? I don't have any takers. Maybe I should just kill Billie first so you girls can watch."

I hear him trying to turn on the light. It doesn't work. *I'm glad I took the light bulb out.*

"How come this damn light switch doesn't work? What did you kids do to it?"

I don't answer him. I just stand at the top of the stairs with Billie's baseball bat and wait for old Frank to reach the top. My first swing at old Frank will be for Daddy!

"I have my knife ready for when I find you. You can't escape from me! It's going to be such a pleasure watching your blood flow all down your young body!"

I hear Frank climb each step. I know the last three steps squeak. He won't be alert enough to worry about any noise. He doesn't know I am ready for him, in the dark, with Billie's bat, at the top of these stairs. *I have to protect my family. I'm not going to let old Frank hurt one more person. He doesn't frighten me anymore!*

Old Frank steps on the first stair that squeaks. I know there is only one more step to go before I'm face-to-face with the devil himself. I can smell Frank's beer breath he is so close. If he reaches the last step that squeaks, I won't have a prayer. I will only be able to hit him in his chest. I have to hit him the minute the second stair squeaks.

I aim Billie's bat ready to strike my target. The second step squeaks. I swing Billie's bat so hard I almost fall face down those stairs in the dark myself. The bat connected with something hard, jerking me backwards.

I hear old Frank land on each step as he tumbles down the stairs. I hope I hit him hard enough he can't get back up and come after me. He will be madder than a bull around a cow in heat with a fence between them if he is still alive. Anyway that's what Roy always tells us when he is mad.

There isn't any noise. Old Frank isn't screaming that he is going to kill us. He hasn't climbed back up the stairs after me. Is he pretending to be hurt or did I really kill him? I wait for a few minutes more before deciding to climb down those dark stairs. There isn't a sound to be heard except my heart pounding. My hands are sweating. I feel like I can't breathe. If old Frank isn't dead, I have to run to Billie and Katie fast. I take Billie's baseball bat with me as I walk down the dark stairs; stepping over old Frank's body. If he is alive, he might grab my leg pulling me down. I will be an easy target. It doesn't matter now. There is no turning back. I step carefully over Frank. He doesn't move. His neck is in a funny position. Blood is oozing out from under him. I thought I only hit his head. His eyes are rolled back into his head. He looks dead! For our safety, I hope so. If he is dead, he won't be able to harm anyone else ever again!

I walk to the living room to see if Sandy is dead. Old Frank cut her throat with his knife. He stabbed her several times with his shiny knife. Her blood is all over the floor. "Oh Sandy, I'll never be able to give you a buggy ride again. I'm so sorry, girl. Thanks for protecting us. I'll never forget you. I promise!"

I run out of the porch to where I left Katie and Billie hiding. Katie grabs me and gives me a big hug. Tears flow down their face.

"We thought you were dead. We heard Frank kill Sandy. We heard every word he screamed at you and poor Sandy. We thought Frank killed you, too."

"Oh, Missy, I'm so glad to see you," Katie says, crying and hugging the life out of me. "Are you hurt? Did he injure you? Where is Frank, Missy?"

"I killed him! He came after me at the top of the stairs. I waited until he reached the top and then I batted his head with Billie's baseball bat. He's lying at the bottom of the stairs with his head in a strange position. There's a lot of blood. Do you think I'll go to jail for murder?"

"No, I don't think so, Missy! Frank said he already killed three people and you were only trying to protect yourself!"

"Do you think he killed Mama?" Billie asks crying.

"I don't know, Billie. He never said he did. We'll just have to wait and see if she shows up," Katie tells him.

"Missy, you're bleeding!" Billie screams.

"No, Billie, it's okay. It's old Frank's blood not mine!"

"Let's go in the house and make sure Frank's dead," Katie suggests.

"No, Katie. I'm pretty sure old Frank's dead. We don't want Billie to see old Frank's bloody body or poor Sandy's. I think we should go to one of the neighbors and call Uncle Riley now. I think he needs to know what happened here tonight. We don't even know if Mama is really alive so it does-n't matter if she gets mad at us for calling him. I sure hope we don't get separated or have to go to the orphanage!"

I feel numb. I'll never be frightened anymore of the dark. Vampires will never be as frightening as old Frank. I will never have to sleep with a pillow or blanket over my head.

The first door we knock on no one answers. The second door we knock on no one answers. We keep knocking on doors until we are a couple of blocks away. Finally, some little old woman answers her door.

"What are you kids doing out at three in the morning? Where is your mother for goodness sake? Does she know you're out at this hour? Oh my, how did you get all of that blood on you, child? Are you okay? Come on in. Let me have a look! Did you have a car accident?"

"No, we had an accident at our house, and I'm okay. Can we use your phone, please?" I ask.

"Sure, honey. You kids want something to drink?"

"That would be real nice, Ma'am. I'm really thirsty. Can I use your bathroom, too?" Billie asks.

"It's down the hall to your right, young man."

"Is this Dixon Police Station? Do you have Chief Riley's phone number? This is Katie Canfield, Dot's daughter. Chief Riley and my mama used to go together and I really need to talk to him. He told us kids we could call him anytime!"

Katie had a hard time convincing the operator to give her Riley's number. But she was insistent and wouldn't give up.

Finally, she convinces the operator to give her his phone number. When she reaches Riley, she tells him everything she knows. He told her he will take care of everything and for us not to worry. He is going to meet us at our house in twenty minutes. We are to stay put until then, if the very kind neighbor will allow us to wait here.

"Sure you kids can stay as long as you need. How about I get you all some blankets. You just sit down on my couch and don't worry about a thing. You're safe with me!"

Chapter Twenty-Three

We wait twenty minutes and head back home. There is enough moonlight left to see each others' faces. I think we all aged a couple of years tonight. Even Billie looks like he has dark circles under his eyes and wrinkles on his little face. It will be different going home without Sandy to greet us. I just hope Mama is able to greet us again.

Sirens blare in the distance. It won't be long before the whole neighborhood is awake. Then they will all know I killed old Frank. I'm not sorry I killed him. He sure wasn't sorry he killed Daddy, Roger, Henry McDougall and Sandy. And he sure wouldn't have felt bad for killing me either. I always knew he didn't like me!

Maybe Uncle Riley won't throw me in jail. I don't want to be in prison with murderers. Everyone says the food is really bad, too. I know I will miss Mama's cooking if she is still alive and ever comes back home again. Maybe she can bring some of her fried chicken or frog legs for me to eat when she visits.

Uncle Riley is the first to arrive at our house. He arrives in twenty minutes just like he promised Katie. He knows how long it takes to get to our house from all his trips to visit Mama.

"Are you kids okay? You sure none of you are hurt?"

"We're fine, Uncle Riley!" Katie tells him, exhausted from no sleep and from stress.

"Come here you kids. Let me give you all a big hug. Just because I'm not going with your Mama anymore doesn't mean I still don't care about you. You'll always be a part of my life. Missy, you have to show me where Frank's body is, sweetheart. Can you go inside with me?"

"I'm okay. I'll show you, but don't make Katie and Billie go inside. Please? I don't want them to see Sandy's and old Frank's bodies. And, Uncle Riley, Frank said he forced Mama's friend Roger off the road the night he was killed. He also said he forced Daddy's car into that telephone pole. He wanted Mama all to himself. And I think I found my daddy's missing wedding band in our study. I was going to ask Mama about it when she returns home, if she ever does!"

"Your Mama will be fine. You know she can take care of herself!" Uncle Riley gave me a hug. "You sure are grown up, Missy. You're not the frightened girl I remember. Come on, I'll follow close behind. I won't let anyone hurt you ever again. Katie, you and Billie can wait in my car. We won't be long."

I show Uncle Riley Sandy's body first. Then I take him to

the bottom of our stairway. Frank hasn't moved. His lifeless body is still where I left it. I almost expected him to get up and scream at me some more waving his knife. There is a pool of blood at the bottom of the stairs where it trickled down the steps. The smell is as bad as when Grandma Irene kills her chickens. The smell of plucking the chickens was about the worst smell ever until I smelled old Frank's blood. This is what death must smell like. But, Henry McDougall didn't smell like this, he had been in the river for days before we found his body. He smelled more like dead fish.

"Where did you put the baseball bat, Missy?" I show Uncle Riley where I left Billie's bat out on our porch. I left it there in case old Frank wasn't really dead and I had to use it on him again to protect us!

Uncle Riley grabs my hand and holds it tight. He walks beside me back to his car where Katie and Billie are waiting. "Missy, it's my pleasure to know such a brave little girl like you. You saved your brother and sister's life tonight!"

I wish I could have saved Sandy's life, too. It is my fault she is dead. I should have never let her loose. Katie was right!

He opens the car door for me and then gets some blankets out of his trunk for us to use to keep warm. "You kids just sit here and take it easy while we go over the scene. You don't need to be frightened any longer. I will take care of you until we find your Mama!"

It isn't long before our whole street is lined with police vehicles, fire trucks, ambulances, and the coroner's van. Our street is lit up with all those lights brighter than a Christmas tree. I even saw a car pull up that said *Dixon Evening Telegraph. I hope they don't find me and take my picture. The last thing we need is some old news reporter flashing his camera in our dirty faces for the entire world to see.*

We have been sitting in Uncle Riley's car a couple of hours when I see two stretchers being wheeled out of our house. One has a bag on it that looks to be the size of a small child. That must be poor Sandy's body. The other stretcher has a white sheet over a large object. Old Frank must be under that sheet. The object is too big to be anything else.

Uncle Riley walks slowly over to his car where we still sit. He waves at me to roll down my window. "Missy, you hitting Frank in the head with the baseball bat isn't what killed him, Hun. When Frank fell backwards, he landed on his own knife. It went clean through his back and straight into that black heart of his. He died instantly. You didn't kill Frank, Missy. I thought you would sleep better knowing!"

We see policemen bringing out plastic bags full of our items. I think one of the items is Billie's wooden baseball bat. *He sure will miss playing with his wood bat. It is the first bat Mama ever bought him.*

Someone is tapping on Uncle Riley's window. It isn't a policeman; the man isn't wearing a hat.

"Katie, are you in there?" We hear someone ask.

Katie turns toward the voice. "Charlie! Oh, Charlie!" She

opens the car door and gives him a big hug. Not being able to hold back her tears any longer, she cries and sobs in his arms while she tells him everything that happened.

He tells her everything will be all right now. It isn't her fault and she shouldn't feel guilty. Frank is to blame, not her. Charlie sits in the car next to Katie telling her how happy he is to find us alive.

But nothing is going to be all right again until Mama comes back home. We all say prayers for Mama's safe return.

We see a car pulling up to our house as the sun is starting to rise. It looks like Mama's car, but there are too many vehicles in the way to be sure.

The coroner begins loading old Frank's body into his van when I hear, "No, not my babies! Where are my babies? Oh God, what happened here, Riley? Don't tell me something has happened to my kids. I'll never forgive myself!" Mama looks like she was about to faint. Some strange man is at her side, holding her up.

"Dot, the kids are all fine. Nothing happened to them. That's Frank's body they're loading into the coroner's van!"

"Frank's? What was he doing here? I told that sorry bastard to pack his bags and move out days ago. He told me he was leaving and moving in with Sam DelRosa yesterday."

"He wasn't too happy with that decision, Dot!" Uncle Riley tells her aggravated.

"Where are my kids, Riley?"

"They're in my car. Go let them know you're all right. Your kids have been through enough stress for a while. At least they can have some relief with you still alive. I'll talk to you later!"

Mama runs to Uncle Riley's car as we open the car doors to greet her. She gives us all a hug and kisses us each over and over.

"Mama, I'm fine! You don't have to kiss me anymore," Billie complains.

Katie looks directly into Mama's eyes. "Where have you been, Mama? We thought old Frank killed you! He was going to kill…"

"Everything is going to be okay from now on. Kids, there's someone I want you to meet. I want you to meet your new dad, Clark Guthrie! We were married yesterday. Isn't that wonderful? You can just call him Uncle Clark!"

"Hi, Uncle Clark, it's nice to meet you," I say, rolling my eyes at Katie and Billie. We all know that no one will ever replace our daddy. And we don't need any strange man to take care of us either. Maybe someday Mama will know it, too. I guess when we asked God to keep Mama safe, we forgot to ask him not to let her bring home any new uncles.

About the Author

Roxe Anne Peacock is the author of LEAVE NO TRACE, two short stories and seven poems. She lives outside Rockford, Illinois with her husband, Tom.

The Rockford Chamber of Commerce sponsored a juried art book, *Art Rockford*, copyright 2004, which Roxe Anne was asked to participate in. It sold at Barnes & Noble and Borders, Rockford Art Museum and at other book venders throughout the Rock River Valley area.

While raising five daughters, she was a Girl Scout leader, 4-H leader and hosted several AFS students.

She participated in Civil War re-enactments for over ten years, helped host ladies' teas for the public, participated in Civil War balls, and helped educate the public at living histories. She also appeared on CSPAN in the Lincoln-Douglas debates.

At the present, Roxe Anne is working on another mystery and a historical cookbook. She enjoys her pug, Spike and being with family and friends.

For your reading pleasure, Roxe Anne Peacock invites you to visit her website to view her mystery, LEAVE NO TRACE, published by Whiskey Creek Press LLC, February 15, 2011.

LEAVE NO TRACE

Jessica Waters was looking forward to attending college in the fall with her best friend, Sandra Adams. But when Sandra disappears the night after prom, mutual friend, Jason Harris becomes the number one suspect. Jason isn't the only suspect in the tight-knit community of Carlsbad, New Mexico. Before Sandra disappeared, she confessed to having an affair with her coach and teacher, Carl Lundstrum. Now Jessica is going to make it her mission to find out what happened if it is the last thing she ever does.

www.whiskeycreekpress.com
Roxe Anne Peacock
www.roxeannepeacock.com